THE RED ARROW MURDERS

A Walter Anchor Ghost Detective Story, Case #6

ROBERT J. MCCARTER

Little Hummingbird Publishing

The Red Arrow Murders

A Walter Anchor Ghost Detective Story

Copyright © 2020 by Robert J. McCarter

Cover image ©Mykhaylo Pelin, 123rf.com

Version 1.0, September 2020

ISBN: 978-1-941153-46-8

Visit Robert's website at: www.RobertJMcCarter.com

Published by:

Little Hummingbird Publishing

P.O. Box 23518

Flagstaff, AZ 86002

❀ Created with Vellum

- **Case 1: Detecting Haley** (also part of *Life After: Stories of Life, Death, and the Places in Between*)
- **Case 2: The Ghost Bride's Gift**
- **Case 3: A Long Hard Fall**
- **Case 4: Death of a Dentist**
- **Case 5: A Hollywood Kind of a Murder**
- **Case 6: The Red Arrow Murders**
- **Unfinished Business: The Cases of Walter Anchor Ghost Detective** (coming October, 2020)

Chapter One

EVERY MURDER MYSTERY HAS TO BEGIN WITH A LIFE ending. By definition.

I don't know about you, but when I was alive, I always loved the predictability of watching murder mysteries, that the bad guy would get caught in the end. There was some comfort in that. But that someone had to die to catalyze that experience, it eventually began to wear on me.

There has to be injustice, of course, for justice to be served. I get that. But does someone have to die every damn week?

"Well, Walter?" Emily asked, looking at our next injustice to right, our next corpse. "What do you think?"

This was standard for Emily. She would find an interesting murder, drag me to it, and try to entice me into solving the case. The weirder the better for her. After all, what are a couple of ghosts supposed to do with their afterlife?

Emily was all smiles, her eyebrows raised expectantly, looking like the four-year-old she was when she died over eighty years ago. She had shoulder-length, curly blond hair, like Shirley Temple, rosy cheeks, shorts, and her usual lollipop-print T-shirt.

She had the enthusiasm of a four-year-old and the jaded love of death of an eighty-year-old ghost.

Since ghostly forms are not fixed and Emily was an advanced ghost with a child's heart, the color of the lollipop was something of a mood ring for her. It was a curious and hopeful yellow. She wanted to engage me in what we both enjoyed doing. How could I turn that down?

I sighed, looking at the mangled body lying on the forest floor. A young man lying facedown, probably in his early twenties. He had been hacked up with a machete or a sword or something like that. Lots of small, precise cuts through his jeans and black T-shirt into his flesh. Slashes on the back of his head through his short brown hair. So many cuts. His blood had stained the dried pine needles red. His arms were splayed out behind him.

Emily had taken us far afield for this one. We were a few hundred miles north of Tucson in the forest just south of Flagstaff, Arizona. This body was by itself with no trail or forest service road in sight.

Someone had hiked out here with him, gone batshit crazy on him with a sharp edge of some sort, and left him to die a slow, horrible death.

There were marks in the pine-needle covered ground, showing him crawling about a dozen feet, leaving a trail of blood while he slowly died.

It seemed like my afterlife was becoming like one of those TV shows. Except Emily with her love of murder could find dead bodies more often than once a week. As often as I let her, really.

"There's no ghost," I said, turning back to the way-too-enthusiastic Emily. "After this, you'd think there'd be a ghost."

She rolled her eyes, her lips twitching into a pout. "Oh, those cases are boring, Walter. We talk to the ghost. Find out who did it. You go type it out at the SECI chamber. The cops arrest them. They go to jail. Blah, blah, blah."

To top it all off, Emily speaks with an adorable lisp turning "cases" into "catheth" and making the incongruity of her young appearance against her love of murder sometimes hard to take. A ghost that looked and sounded like an adorable little girl loving murder so very much.

The SECI chamber is that typewriter for ghosts that was invented at the University of Arizona in Tucson. It is what I am typing on right now. It is the piece of technology that lets ghosts be detectives and bring people to justice. Otherwise we'd be solving murders and not being able to do anything about it, and that would just suck.

I sighed and nodded. She was right, of course, a ghost could sometimes make cases so easy it was boring, but I didn't have to like it. And I didn't have to like wading into another screwed-up human circumstance either.

I think this has become a bit of a ritual for us. Joyful Emily finds a murder so bizarre it makes my head hurt. I get grumpy and protest too much. Emily launches a charm offensive that eventually wins me over and we take on the case. Blah, blah, blah.

I was tired of that happening every "week" too.

So I decided to mix it up.

"Wow!" I said, my voice actually containing some energy. "This is wonderfully strange, Emily. You did good, kid, finding this poor boy. Let's get to work and find the murderer and bring them to justice!"

I was trying to be enthusiastic, but it came out a little bit weird. Well, a lot weird. I used to be an actor, I could have done it convincingly, but I didn't. It came out stilted and awful.

"What is wrong with you, Walter?" Emily asked, her head cocked to one side and her fists on her hips.

"Nothing, honey," I said, digging in deeper with the faux enthusiasm. "I just want to solve this murder. Let's get to it!"

I turned around, slowly taking in our surroundings. Which was trees. So many trees. And pine needles. And downed branches. And pinecones, from new nut-brown cones to grey rotting cones. And volcanic rocks with pale grey lichen on them. The body was in the middle of a small clearing of trees.

Flagstaff is in the middle of the largest ponderosa pine forest in the world. It's a massive forest where almost all the trees are ponderosas. There are some scattered oaks, most of them pretty scraggly, and aspen and fir at higher elevations, but around here it's all pine trees. Endless damn pine trees. One part of the forest looking much like another part if there are no landmarks visible.

I flew straight up about two hundred feet and rotated around again. I could see highway 89A cutting through a valley to the east. It goes from Flagstaff to Sedona. The land was undulating and rough, the result of uneven erosion in the rocky land. The earth here is all volcanic, the San Francisco Peaks, which I could see to the north, was once a massive volcano and built up the north country.

"Walter?" Emily called from down below.

She didn't fly up but stayed on the ground. As the saying went around the graveyard in Tucson, "If you act like you're alive, you feel more like you are alive." And I get that. It's good hygiene for ghosts, helps you stay stable without a body. But who wants to be a ghost and not fly around sometimes?

"What are you doing, Walter?" she called.

"Just getting the lay of the land," I said. "Why the hell would anyone ever come out here?"

"You know… to hike," Emily said in a very youthful and condescending tone. "Fresh air. Exercise. Stuff like that."

A groan escaped me despite trying to stay cheerful about this. I was never much of a hiker. When I was an actor, keeping in shape was part of the job description, and even afterward as a dentist I kept it up. But at a gym. Where things are civilized. Away from bugs and snakes and bears. Where pine needles and pinecones can't poke you.

My ex-wife Sun did like to hike, but in exotic locations with beautiful views. I'd doggedly hike with her since the view when she was in front of me was always a good one.

But thoughts of Sun just soured my mood. It hadn't been easy, but Sun and I had repaired things a lot while Emily and I were investigating the death of the ghost bride. But Sun was the one that got away and it was not like we could have much of a relationship now. I am not a haunter. Definitely not one of those ghosts.

"So where's the trail?" I asked Emily. "I don't see any trail. There's a dirt road about half a mile away, but that's it."

Emily sighed, loudly and petulantly. "Please come get me, Walter. I want to see."

Emily and I were not quite at our best. I had been digging around my past a lot lately and it just made me grumpy… well, "grumpier." I'm not one of those ghosts having a good time in their afterlife. I feel like I have a job to do, that "unfinished business" and all. And I figure that my unfinished business is my own murder, but the leads ran out a while ago, and recently… well, let's just say it's gotten complicated.

I slowly lowered myself to the ground, putting in some

effort so my long trench coat flared out around me like I was really passing through the air. A little drama that made it take longer than it needed to.

Emily raised one eyebrow and shook her head. If anybody knew me, it was Emily. And she knew this was my little passive aggressive version of a fit.

Four-year-olds are really better at them. They don't hold back or pretend it's not happening, they just let loose and you know what they are upset about.

Adults? Not so much.

"You ready to tell me what's going on?" Emily asked when I got to the ground.

"Nope," I said. And I wasn't.

I reached down and picked her up. So ghosts can see and hear, really well. But they can't smell, they can't taste, and touch... well, it's barely there and you have to do it right. And I did. I matched the frequency of my ghostly form to Emily's—basically making my form neater and less transparent—and took her in my arms.

The ghostly sense of touch is a barely there, almost numb feeling, but it is actually very important. I can live without the sense of smell and taste—yeah, I get grumpy about that too—but touch is essential to being human. It really is. Touch is the sensation that lets you know you are not alone in this world.

And maybe that is what Emily was doing, in part, by having me fly her up. She's a wily old ghost and well skilled. She knows what it takes to survive as a ghost and she does a lot of little things to keep me stable.

Like have me help her solve murders.

All the time.

I took her slowly up into the clear blue sky. That's the one thing I'll say about the high country, the air is clean and the sky is so blue it almost doesn't look real.

I took us up about two hundred feet and Emily said, "I thought so." She was looking straight down at the victim.

"What?" I asked.

She pointed. "See the arrow, Walter?"

And I did. The kid had dragged himself bleeding across the forest floor making a long red stain and his hands were back behind him at about 45-degree angles turning his body and the blood stain into an arrow.

The arrow pointed to the northeast, towards Flagstaff. But…

"That can't mean anything," I said.

"Why not?" Emily asked, her pale blue eyes full of challenge.

"Well… we're far enough away from Flagstaff that he would have to be a human compass or something to point to anything. And even if he was, the whole of Flagstaff is mostly in that direction. How would we know what he's pointing at?"

She pursed her lips. "Well, then you explain it, Mr. Smartypants." It came out as "Thmartypanth," taking a bit of the sting out.

I opened my mouth, but didn't speak right away. My faux cheerfulness was gone, and probably for the better, but I couldn't believe she was even asking me this.

"He was dying, Em. He used his last bits of energy trying to get to help. His arms just ended up that way."

She sighed and nodded. "But it's a lead, Walter. While it might not be anything, it could be something."

I just stared at her.

"Come on," she said, putting some punch in her young voice. "You're Walter Anchor, ghost detective. You can't let a mystery like this go."

This was not looking like a very fun case to me.

Chapter Two

WE DIDN'T GO FOLLOW THE ARROW. NOT YET. I FLEW US much higher, several thousand feet up, so we could get a better sense of where the arrow pointed and look for any other anomalies.

The blood had turned rather dark and flies were all over the corpse, so we knew the death wasn't fresh. Which was a bit unlike Emily. She often got us to murders shortly after they happened. She had a sixth sense for these kinds of things.

I sometimes wished she could sense murders before they happened. But that's not the kind of thing I ever said to her. She would take it like a four-year-old and it wouldn't go well. And we have the talents we have, after all.

She's good at finding murders. I'm good at being grumpy.

We didn't find anything interesting up high, so I flew us back down and we started taking a closer look at the crime scene.

"Where's his backpack?" I asked, slowly walking around the scene. Being ghosts we didn't have to worry about contaminating evidence or stepping in the blood or smelling the corpse, which must be starting to get ripe right about now.

Emily shrugged.

"He wouldn't be out here without a water bottle, at least, right?" I asked. Not being much of a hiker, it really was a question.

Emily shrugged again. What would a girl who died at the age of four really know about hiking anyway? Did people even call it "hiking" eighty-some years ago?

"And the shoes," I said, pointing. They were black canvas sneakers. Not hiking boots. Crappy tread. "Those aren't hiking boots."

Another shrug.

Crap. The silent treatment. I had told her I had discovered something in my past but wasn't ready to talk about it. That had been a good step, but I hadn't told her about it yet and it was still this barrier between us.

I much preferred her loud and angry than quiet and sulky.

I sighed and just ignored Emily, squatting low and looking closely at the body. This is an area where we were way better than humans. Great eyesight. No creaky knees. No getting barfy because we can't smell.

The pants were plain old blue jeans but were very worn with a few holes in them and they looked super dirty, like they hadn't been washed in way too long. I glanced at the face and from what I could see from the side, confirmed that he was in his early twenties. The T-shirt had holes in it too and, given the coolness of early fall, he was way underdressed. The shirt was black fading to charcoal from too many trips through the washer and there was some faded silk screening on the front that I couldn't see enough of to even hazard a guess.

Emily seemed to have gotten bored with giving me the silent treatment and was doing the same thing I was. Getting close. Looking hard. Mentally cataloging details.

She really does love murder. She might be mad at me, but she was still driven to solve this case. Any case, really. The living are driven by their biology to get out there and do things. You have to. The biology can't be ignored for too long.

The dead have to find other ways to keep active, because being active is essential to being sane.

"How did he get out here?" I asked. "I don't think he walked all the way here."

Emily's green eyes darkened and narrowed as she studied me. She straightened up on the other side of the corpse and folded her little arms across her chest. "I don't think I want to solve a murder today."

I shrugged, pretending not to understand what she was getting at. "Okay. I bet he'll be here tomorrow. What do you have in mind?"

Her nostrils flared and she shook her head. While she knew I had found something in my past, and while she had told me it was okay to have secrets, that we all had secrets, this one had started to fester and I knew it. But still I couldn't do anything about it.

This wasn't me just being grumpy. She didn't have any problem with that. In fact, I think she liked it. She could counteract the grumpy Walter with the exuberant Emily. I think she liked it like that, it gave her an excuse to be so exuberant.

Maybe she thought I owed her the truth here—she had

saved me, after all. I had been a dentist. Murdered in one of my own dental chairs with an overdose of propofol, a drug I had some unfortunate recreational experience with, so it was ruled a suicide. I had ended up haunting my old practice, unable to leave, and then haunting my office manager, Midge. Emily had found me, barely holding on, in the bathroom with poor Midge. I was desperate. I thought Midge was the key to my murder. I didn't leave her side until Emily came along and taught me how to be a proper ghost.

Ghosts who don't find something to do, don't find a way to be in balance, end up slipping into their regrets and reliving all their mistakes in a place the ghosts in Tucson call the bardo.

And yes, Emily saved me. And yes, I owed her. And so I remade myself into a detective, with a trench coat and a fedora no less, and have been learning to solve murders.

And part of it had been selfish, thinking that if I got good enough at this, I'd be able to solve my own murder, finish my unfinished business and "move on."

But I had a lead, I had a suspect, and I had enough experience now to figure it out. But I couldn't do anything about it. I couldn't see my past erode even further like it had every time I had gone looking at it.

I was a ghost and I was the one being haunted, by how I died, by the life I had lived, by all the things I had missed while I was alive.

Emily was staring at me, her arms still crossed, her eyes narrow, watching my face, probably picking up half of what I was feeling. With the density of flesh gone, ghosts are more than a little intuitive. But they aren't mind readers. Emily knew something was up with me but didn't know what.

"Yeah, I'm not feeling it today," she said, her voice the growl of an old woman.

With a pop, she was gone and I was left there in the middle of the forest with a dead body and the trail of blood behind it forming something of an arrow pointing toward Flagstaff.

Chapter Three

I KEPT INVESTIGATING.

This was becoming something of a pattern for us. She had found the Hollywood murder case and left me there, thinking that since I had wanted to be an actor, maybe I was better off in Hollywood.

She had found this one with her usual exuberance and I had just gotten weird with my false enthusiasm and driven her away.

And this was a bizarre murder case, just the kind of thing Emily likes the best, so I knew it was bad.

I couldn't "pop" like Emily and go instantly from place to place. I had to fly and I wasn't in the mood to fly back to Tucson and try to find Emily and try to make it right. She might not be there. She could be anywhere in the world.

And I was more than a little bit worried about her. About us. She loves solving cases more than anything. Which meant something serious was going on. This growing pattern was not a good thing.

It wasn't much of a decision on my part, I just pretended Emily had gone off to get us help or something and kept looking. I followed the bloody trail back to its origin and found an area where feet had scuffed through the layers of dead pine needles and crunched some fallen pinecones. There had been a fight of some sort. There were also small splats of blood on the ground a few feet away.

So the victim and the assailant had struggled. Maybe the edged weapon hadn't come out at first.

I flew up a few feet and looked down, trying to see if I could detect a pattern in the markings.

The forest floor was thick with dead pine needles, so it takes a lot to disturb them. Just walking across them won't do much. There were a few spots where their feet dug all the way to the ground.

I flew up a little higher and it became clearer. The scuffs radiated out in an irregular wandering pattern. There had been shoving. Close to a pine tree was smaller scuff. Someone had fallen and their feet had dug in when they levered themselves up.

So either hard shoves or punches were thrown.

I flew down to the ground and looked over the area closely, hoping to find something that was dropped. And sure enough under a scuff of pine needles was an open penknife.

I couldn't move it, of course, but I could sink into the ground and get my head close to it. I don't cast a shadow and don't actually have eyes, so I could get close enough that it was like I had a magnifying glass.

The knife was old, the edge a bit mangled by someone who really didn't know how to sharpen it. It was a cheap knife with a faux wood plastic handle, the blade about three and a half inches long. The blade was clean, not a bit of blood, and my heart sank.

If there had been blood, that would have probably

been from the perp and the police could take it from here and I could leave this poor dead kid with a good conscience.

But no blood. No easy answers. And no Emily's endless enthusiasm.

I sighed and kept looking.

I TRACED BACK FROM THE SCUFFED AREA. WHILE walking doesn't do much to the thick layer of pine needles deposited over many seasons, it does do something. I spend hours studying the forest floor and getting a feel for the normal variations and then going back to the scuffed area trying to see if I could tell which way they came from.

No trails here. No roads closer than half a mile. If they were the only ones to walk here, I should be able to find it.

But finding the trail was not some romantic, look here's a broken twig, and over there is a bent branch or a bit of cloth like you might see in the movies. This was slow and arduous and very boring, but slight, smaller scuffs were there. I could only pick them up occasionally, but I could find them.

It was this strange, nearly meditative state. The forest floor was all there was to me. The natural variants, the animal trails that disturbed in a thin line, the small volcanic rocks with pale green lichen clinging to it, the scuffs from our perp and vic.

The arrow was pointing to the northeast, so I expected the trail to go to the southwest, deeper into the forest, but it didn't. It quickly curved around and headed east. To the dirt road.

This took the rest of the day. I kept slipping out of my zen state and worrying about Emily, wondering how I would even survive my afterlife without her, but being terrified to tell her my secret. And then I would lose the trail and it would take me time to get my mind in the right state and I would have to backtrack.

Under the robin's-egg blue sky in the thick forest, it was a long and awful day. I kept expecting Emily to come back, but she didn't.

We had had our misunderstandings, of course we had. But it was often the four-year-old that got hurt and that was easy enough to rectify. This time it was the eighty-year-old ghost that was hurt, and this wasn't going to be simple and it wasn't going to be easy.

And I was quite sure that I was going to have to tell her my secret and that would just make things worse.

As the sun was edging close to the horizon, I tracked the perp and vic back to the dirt road and found some fresh tire tracks.

The perp had driven him out here, marched him through the forest, fought him, and then cut him time and time again until he slowly bled out while dragging himself across the forest floor and leaving his arms arranged like an arrow with his dying breath.

Yeah. I don't think so.

I have been doing this long enough to know that when you hit something in a case that just doesn't make sense then you are missing a piece of data or have made a wrong assumption.

There are exceptions, of course. Humans are far less rational than we like to pretend we are, but I had something wrong here, something very wrong.

I WALKED BACK TO THE BODY, ALONG THE COURSE I HAD

tracked, just in case I might have missed something. I went to the scuffed area and tried to recreate the fight, but it was chaotic enough that I couldn't say it was much more than a fight. But I walked through it anyway in case some details fell out.

I felt silly referring to them as "perp" and "vic" so I gave them names—Paul and Vince—as I thought it through.

So Paul and Vince walked out here for some reason heading mostly west and then shortly after they turned to the northeast they started fighting. Shoving, shouting. Maybe they were fighting over a girl or a job or a bet. Anyway, just shoving at first. And then Paul shoved Vince too far and he stumbled back and landed by the tree. He was losing, being the weaker of the two, and pulled out his penknife and threatened Paul with it.

Paul, not being a dummy, picked up one of the many branches lying around and hit Vince's arm with it, knocking the knife away. The fight escalated then to blows and then... Paul pulled a sharp-edged weapon and started slicing Vince up with vicious precision?

Yeah, that makes no sense. None at all. How does a scuffle escalate into a cruel killing? A stabbing, sure. Someone falling and smashing their head on one of the many rocks around here, absolutely. But delivering dozens and dozens of shallow cuts, no way.

The sun was down by now, but that didn't matter to me. I could see just fine in low light and I kept going.

I decided to assume the fight was staged or incidental. In other words, I no longer believed the fight was a catalyst to the murder, and if it wasn't, then...?

Then the murder had been premeditated. Paul had brought Vince out here to kill him. Maybe the fight had been a defensive one initiated by Vince.

I went back to the body. Something about it was really bugging me. I looked at the arms and they were straight, palms up, and back from his body forming a perfect arrowhead.

And then it hit me.

Vince didn't put his arms that way with his dying breath—Paul had arranged them that way.

Paul had arranged the whole thing. Bringing Vince out here. Cutting him and arranging his arms so he looked like an arrow, especially from above. Somehow getting Vince to crawl in a straight line while he bled out.

A chill ran through me although I lacked a body, and I looked around, suddenly afraid I was being watched. This murder had been premeditated and cruel, designed to leave Vince looking exactly like he does. Like a big red arrow in the forest pointing towards Flagstaff.

If I had had a stomach I would have thrown up.

This was not like the other murders we had solved. This was not like anything we'd seen. And this case went beyond the little squabble Emily and I were having.

I flew up into the sky, because I couldn't stand being next to the corpse anymore, but then I could see the dark red blood trail edging towards black in the quickly darkening night. I turned away and looked south towards Tucson and did the only thing I could think of doing.

"Emily!" I screamed. "I need you, Emily. I need you right now!"

Chapter Four

Earlier I mentioned that ghosts are more intuitive once the flesh is gone—like Emily and her sixth sense about bizarre murders. As ghosts spend a lot of time together, just like when people spend a lot of time together, they can have intuitive incidents, somehow knowing something about the other that doesn't involve the five senses.

Well, ghosts with their enhanced intuition are even more so. Emily always seemed to know when I was in trouble, when I was teetering on the edge. When I really, really needed her.

That's what I was doing six hundred feet above the corpse arranged as an arrow pointing towards Flagstaff, Arizona. I was hoping that Emily wasn't too mad to pay attention to her intuition. I needed help on this case and I needed it now.

And my own ghostly intuition was telling me... well, it wasn't actually telling me anything coherent, I was just freaked out and paranoid and worried that the killer was watching me.

Ignore for a moment the fact that the killer was alive

and I was not and couldn't possibly be watching me. I "felt" like he was. It felt dangerous. I felt vulnerable.

So I screamed for Emily. Not "at the top of my lungs" because I didn't have any lungs. I also didn't have any vocal cords to get worn out so I just threw a fit and screamed and screamed and screamed.

Unbecoming, yes, I know. Looking at Emily and me, you would assume that I was the parent in the relationship. After all, I look to be in my forties and she looks to be around four. But Emily has had consciousness for over eighty-five years and I knew that her feelings towards me tended toward the maternal.

All that said, I screamed. A lot. "Emily. I need you. I need you now! Emily!"

But she didn't reply, so I changed my tune. "I'm sorry, okay. Do you hear me, Emily? I'm sorry. I've been keeping something from you, something big. I know you know this, I told you as much in Hollywood, but what you don't know is that I have a good reason for not sharing it. It would change everything and I…" I wasn't shouting anymore, just talking. It wasn't the volume that counted as much as the emotion. "I don't know that I want things to change.

"Emily. Please. Something terrible happened to this boy and I can't do this on my own. I can't do this without you."

Still nothing. Just the buzz of cars going down 89A and the glow of Flagstaff beating away the growing darkness as the stars popped out above me.

Screw it then.

I would do this without her. I would fly back to the graveyard and grab some of the ghosts that help us with tough cases who Emily has named "Anchor's Irregulars." The reference to Sherlock Holmes and his "Baker Street Irregulars" was more than a little bit embarrassing to me. I was no Holmes. I was just a washed-out actor who became a dentist and only started on this detective thing to solve my own murder.

And there's the rub. My own murder.

At Emily's encouragement, I recently went and wrote all about my last days alive, all that was happening, all that I remembered. Ghosts have fantastic memories and the act of writing can really pull details out. There had been a lot I had been ignoring, clues I hadn't remembered. But writing about my last day and about haunting my practice brought it all back.

I was pretty sure I knew who killed me.

I just had to prove it.

And once I did, once I finished my proverbial "unfinished business" I could "move on."

Just like the living, us ghosts aren't real sure what is next, but it seems to be a pleasant thing from all reports.

"Emily," I said softly. "Please, you've got to understand. I think I know who killed me. I might know why. And if we prove it, I'll… I'll…"

I couldn't finish, but I didn't have to.

With a "pop" Emily was there hovering over the dark forest, tears streaming down her round face, her green eyes wide.

Emily and I are a strange match, but we had found something unusual living or dead, a working and loving partnership. I was having trouble conceiving of my existence without her, but I truly did not like being a ghost. I wanted to move on even though what was next was a big mystery. My life felt like it had been a bit like I was being tossed around in a dryer. My afterlife had been wading into the darker side of humanity. And while I loved Emily, I was ready for a more peaceful existence, and "moving on" felt like it was that.

Emily sniffed, still studying my face. Had she heard me? Maybe she had been close enough all along. Was her finely tuned intuition enough that she got the essential details now that I had spoken them? It didn't matter, it was clear from her stricken face that she knew.

And then her lips formed a thin line and she took a deep breath, her face slowly hardening.

It only took a few seconds, but it was a bit frightening. The four-year-old who wears her emotions on her sleeve was subsumed by the eighty-year-old ghost that had seen way the hell too much. The hard look of the eighty-year-old ghost on her four-year-old face was so incongruous as to be disturbing.

"What did you find out about him?" she asked, her chin pointing down to the corpse, a dark spot in the dark-ening night that pointed towards Flagstaff.

Chapter Five

Because Emily died at the age of four, she never lost the child in her, even through all the decades dead. It was what made her so unique and special... and often baffling and infuriating.

It was what was most essential about her, that tug of war between her vastly different selves. Sometimes as crotchety as can be and a few seconds later a joyful little imp.

But that was not the Emily that went to work with me that day. She still looked like a four-year-old with her blond Shirley Temple curls and white T-shirt with big lollipop print, but there was no child in her manner and a growl in her voice.

The traditionally cheerful lollipop on her T-shirt, which was a reflection of her mood, was a dark, dingy purple. I had never seen that color before. I wasn't sure what it reflected other than a dark mood.

She was focused on the murder and it was abundantly clear that she did not want to discuss my own murder and the prospect of me moving on.

And you might think that would have been fine by me, after all, I had been the one keeping it a secret, but now that the proverbial cat was out of the bag and I knew it couldn't be stuffed back in, I wanted to talk about it.

I followed Emily down to the forest floor. It was fully dark and the moon wasn't up, but starlight still works fine for ghosts. Our eyeless sight is remarkably adaptable. It's not like we could see as well as in full daylight, but we could still see.

I showed her the carefully arranged arms, palms up at just the right angle. I showed her where they scuffled and the fallen knife. I took her along their path back to the road and showed her the recent tire tracks.

She was quiet the whole time, asking questions with as few syllables as needed. Her face a grim mask of determination that was incongruous with her adorable four-year-old form.

"Conclusions?" she asked after I had shown it all and we had walked back to the body.

This, too, was unusual behavior. Emily generally acted as the catalyst in cases, letting me take the lead, although I often suspected that she knew a lot more than she was letting on, allowing me to go through the motions as a way to teach me and to keep me busy. That single-word question was like Holmes querying Watson to make sure he had followed the clues properly.

"The murder was premediated," I said. "The goal was to leave the corpse looking like this, like an arrow, especially from above so that…" I trailed off.

"Continue," she said, her hands on her hips, her jaw set.

"The arrow is meant to be seen from above." I turned to the northeast, the direction the arrow was pointing. "The airport is over there. Maybe planes fly over this land, maybe it was meant to be spotted by them, but…"

She sighed. "But what?"

I didn't like this new Emily. Not a bit.

"I… I just have a feeling. I think we were meant to find this. I think someone did this, arranged this body for you and me."

Her jaw dropped open and her green eyes went wide and she suddenly looked like a terrified four-year-old. Her head snapped around looking at the tall, dark trees that seemed ominous now in the dark.

"Walter…" she began, her voice almost shaking. "But that… I…"

I nodded. "I know, honey. That means someone has been reading my stories. Just like that ghost we came across on the Hollywood case. I think what we have been doing is influencing the living. Someone believes my stories. And that someone is now toying with us and they took a life to get our attention."

She swallowed hard and shook her head. "But that is a big leap. A giant leap. People on the ground would notice he was arranged as an arrow."

I nodded. She was right. "One good rain or even a little snow and this doesn't look nearly as much like an arrow. The ravens have been at the body, but once the coyotes find it, it won't be an arrow anymore. And how long before someone stumbles upon this body? No trail, no close roads. We are in the middle of a huge forest."

She bit her lip and nodded.

"I might be wrong about this," I said. "Maybe this whole thing is just creeping me out. But how about we assume we were meant to find this? That the murderer knows your ability to find bizarre murders and that you and I are running around trying to solve them."

"Yeah… okay." She took a deep breath, her face hardening again. "You stay here, I'll get the Irregulars and we'll have one of them watch the body and—"

"Two," I said, interrupting her. "Two of them watching the body. I don't want to leave anyone out here alone for long."

She nodded. "Two to watch the body, and then I'll take you to the SECI chamber and you can type up enough to get law enforcement out here and then…" she trailed off.

I sighed. "And then we follow the clue left for us, we follow the arrow and try to figure out what it is pointing at."

The wind whipped up, rattling the branches around us and Emily happily popped away to get help and I shoved my fears down and kept an eye on our victim Vince.

Chapter Six

I⟩t was one thing being a ghost, being invisible to the living world and going around and solving murders. It was something completely different knowing that there are living people doing things *because* you are dead and solving murders.

This boy, "Vince," might have been killed just to get our attention. And let me tell you, that will mess with your mind, living or dead.

While we got a tiny taste of this with the Hollywood case, this was something else entirely.

I was hoping Emily would be gone for a minute or two, that she would pop back with a couple of other ghosts and I could get the hell out of here. But it wasn't quick. Emily was honest, she told them what we thought we were up against and, well… who really wants to volunteer for that? To go from an invulnerable ghost to…

There was so much I didn't know and my mind just went wild. If our perp, "Paul," was doing this to get our attention, that meant he had read my stories, studied my methods, thought this through and planned it. But what was the goal? To try to outsmart the ghost detectives or to do something a lot more sinister.

My creeped-out factor said Paul was trying to do both.

If I didn't think much of the forest before, I really hated it now, all dark and foreboding. Trees groaning in the wind. Branches snapping and falling. Clouds rolling in to cover the stars and blot out the little light we had.

After an hour of this, I shook it off and stopped just standing around. It wasn't good for me, not at all. My biology was gone, what could the living possibly do to me?

I started examining the body again, even though the light was getting worse. I sank into the ground so I was eye-level with him and looked at every square inch of our victim. It took longer in the near darkness, but I could still do it. And I found some things.

His right palm had a fresh scrape which lined up with the scuffed-up pine needles and the dropped knife.

His head was turned to the right and I saw a slight bruise on his right cheek. Again, the fight was looking more and more real.

And then I found a needle mark on his right arm.

At first, I thought maybe he was a drug user, that might explain his unkempt appearance, but there was only one and it was recent.

Maybe he had a recent blood test, but it looked like the needle gage was too small for that.

Or maybe Paul injected Vince with something. Before the fight? After the fight? Before they even came out here?

I could only guess, but it certainly complicated the picture.

If we assume that the injection was part of what happened here, what could the murderer possibly gain? Whatever it was, it couldn't be good.

The distraction had been good, but now I was even more creeped out than ever.

———

I GO TO THE SECI CHAMBER AND WRITE UP THESE CASES for a couple of reasons. The first is so the police have something to go on and can arrest the killer. The second is because I need to write these cases. Call it therapy. I am still quite human, despite the lack of biology, and these experiences take some sorting through.

I understand that Tamara Watson and Jin Shi, who run Afterlife Communications, have been publishing our stories, making money off of them to fund what they are doing. And I never had a problem with that, but now…?

If this killing was done to get our attention, that feels like a violation, like someone is using what they know against me, like they know things they shouldn't, private things.

And I guess this blurring of the line between the living and the dead was inevitable with what Tamara and Jin are doing. And in some ways that is the whole point. If you know that death is not the end, does that change how you live?

If I am right, that did indeed change how our perp, Paul, has lived. It has channeled his murderous tendencies in my direction. Not exactly the kind of reaction you are hoping for when you imagine how the assurance of an afterlife will affect the living.

I had way too much time to think about all of this while the clouds sped above and the wind blew and the trees creaked and the night crawled on.

After I had examined the body, I just paced in a slow circle around it, trying to keep my emotions in check.

When Emily popped back in, I jumped, so lost I was in my own thoughts. She had Anna-Maria with her, a young Hispanic woman with long black hair arranged in a braid, a round face, and an easy smile. She wore a leather jacket, jeans, and tall black boots like she was ready to jump onto a Harley.

"Where's Fredrick? Where's Blinky?" I asked. They were the other two that were regularly part of the Irregulars.

Emily pursed her lips and shook her head.

"I don't know what they are scared of," Anna-Maria said loudly, louder than she needed to. "Is this the stiff?" She took a step towards "Vince" and her lips puckered into a sour expression.

I nodded. "What happened?" I asked Emily.

She shrugged. "Things, in general, have gotten wonky lately with more and more of the living believing in us. First all the lookie-loos at the graveyard and then the protests at the Afterlife Communications offices." She sighed. "Folks are a bit spooked. I talked to Fredrick first and he begged off, saying he needed to stay at the grave-yard, and then I couldn't find Blinky."

I could imagine it. Emily telling Fredrick what we suspected that there was a murder committed just to get our attention. You've never seen a grapevine where word travels as fast as a graveyard and I bet Blinky got word and got lost.

"Wimps," Anna-Maria said with a jab of her chin. "I ain't afraid of the living."

I sighed. I really hadn't wanted to leave someone here alone. As I could attest, this idea could really worm its way around your head and get to you.

"Thank you, Anna-Maria," I said. "I really appreciate it. We won't be long."

She shrugged and it looked casual but her brown eyes were a bit too wide. I can't pop, and with the delay we had already had, I wanted to get to the SECI chamber and write this up. I would send Emily, but she is the world's slowest typer and she would be at it for hours.

Anna-Maria died while rock climbing. She used to ride motorcycles and had gotten herself arrested protesting on the border. She was young and brash and as tough as they come, but I was worried about leaving her out here alone.

I shook my head trying to clear it. I had just spooked myself. The living were no threat to us.

"Let's go," I said to Emily, and she grabbed my arm and popped us away.

Chapter Seven

I SHOULD HAVE SENT EMILY BACK TO BE WITH ANNA-Maria while I typed but I didn't want Emily out there either. Her looking like a cute four-year-old still messes with my mind because she's old and tough and probably the most skilled ghost around the graveyard.

But she didn't volunteer either, which was telling.

She popped us to the 2.0 version of the SECI chamber. They are getting ready with a portable 3.0 version, but this one is reserved for me and a few other ghosts and is in a secret location.

There are a lot of ghosts out there that want to be heard, and even though not all of them can manage to type on these, the well-known SECI chambers tend to be crowded.

The SECI chamber works on the principle that ghosts emanate high-frequency electromagnetic (EM) radiation. The chamber is a bit larger than a phone booth and shielded from external EM radiation and has a big keyboard on the wall with a monitor above it. The keys detect ghostly EM radiation when you poke your finger through and the monitor displays what you are writing.

The hard part is that that high-frequency EM radiation that it detects is a much lower frequency than is natural for us ghosts. That's why it's hard to do and takes so much concentration.

As Emily watched, I got to it, typing out the basics of what we had found.

"So… you know who your murderer is," Emily said quietly once I was about a paragraph in.

Her tone was calm. Even. Not the joyfully inquisitive tone of a four-year-old or the growl of a jaded eighty-year-old.

"Yes… well, maybe," I said, trying to stay focused on my task. It was clear now that Emily didn't pop back to Anna-Maria not because she was afraid but because she wanted to talk to me. "I've got motive and opportunity."

She nodded and sighed. The chamber was not big so she was right next to me.

"And when did you figure this out?" she asked, again her tone neutral.

I didn't answer her right away. I kept on typing for a while. It was clear this was going to be a thing, a big thing, but this murder was more than a little disturbing and we needed help.

"A couple of months," I finally said when I was almost done.

"When you went and wrote about your last days?" she asked.

She already knew this. I had told her as much on the Hollywood case. Things had been getting tense between us and I felt I needed to explain my shift in mood.

I nodded and kept typing, the tension in the small space nearly palpable.

"After you were done," she said, her voice still calm, "you told me you didn't find any new leads."

I nodded. "I'm sorry, Emily. I just couldn't face it."

It wasn't enough. Expression of sorrow always seems to be so hollow when you've hurt someone you care about.

"I understand," she said, but I knew she didn't. She couldn't. I hadn't bothered to explain it.

"It was… I…" I stammered, staring down at Emily, her face slack. I opened my mouth to say more but she raised her hand and cut me off.

"I need some air," she said quietly and walked through the SECI chamber wall.

A ghost never needs air.

I bit my lip and got back to my typing.

Chapter Eight

IT TOOK LONGER THAN I HAD HOPED TO TYPE UP THINGS at the SECI chamber. Emily distracted me with her questions. I was still spooked by the murder, my paranoia going so far as to wondering if they knew about this location, if they were watching us here.

Not that they could watch us. We were ghosts. The fact that the SECI chamber could detect our EM radiation enough to let us type things like this was something of a miracle.

But what if someone had figured it out, how to broaden that technology and learned how to detect the super high-frequency EM radiation that ghosts emitted? Then a ghost would be visible.

My head just wasn't on right. I stood alone in the SECI chamber after I was done, after I had typed the secret "911" code at the end of the document to get Tamara's attention so she could pass it on to law enforcement. I just stood there, my mind racing.

It had been a joy to most of us to be able to communicate from beyond our biological existences, but the world was changing because of it. It had to. This murder, if my paranoia was right, being one of many changes.

I also paused because I didn't want to deal with Emily. With the secret I had kept. With her disappointment in me. It was all just too much.

I wasn't even a detective. I mean, I was living my after-life as one, but I had no real training, although my time as an actor made me comfortable with improvisation and faking my way through things.

But I couldn't fake my way through my friendship with Emily, and the murder we were dealing with deserved better than that too.

I shook my head and tried to shove all of that down. There was no time for this, not for any of this.

Emily was no nonsense when I walked out of the chamber and I was grateful. She grabbed my arm and popped us back to Anna-Maria without a word.

The clouds had thickened and the night had grown darker. We popped in about a dozen feet from the corpse and I saw several figures hunched over it.

Several.

At first, I thought that the body had been found, but these people glowed with a light of their own and were slightly transparent. Ghosts.

And then I realized that Anna-Maria was not there. All three figures were men.

Emily, who still had a hold of my arm, must have noticed the same thing. She squeezed. It was the numb, barely there sensation of a ghost, but the meaning was still the same.

When I was alive, I was a dentist. The boss of my office. I was not used to people messing with my things, and after the shock wore off, I got angry.

"What's going on here?" I asked, sounding like nothing other than a parent talking to their children.

"Ah…" one of them began, standing up. "If it isn't Casablanca Walter and little baby Emily."

He went by Galt and he had small grey eyes and his quirking smile revealed crooked teeth. His stringy black hair was shoulder length and he was dressed all in black, simple pants and a long-sleeved shirt looking rather goth-ish. He was flanked by two other young male ghosts dressed about the same.

We were not friends, to say the least. Back on my first case, he had been the one who taught Haley to hurt the living. She almost killed her murderer with what Galt taught her. I still missed Haley who was up in Utah at another graveyard where things are a lot quieter and a lot simpler than they are in Tucson.

His Casablanca reference was to my trench coat and fedora. It was at the end of that first case that Emily in her enthusiasm had talked me into changing my ghostly form so I looked like a 1940s-era detective.

"Mind telling me what you boys are doing here?" I asked, keeping my tone even.

Emily gave my arm another squeeze. "Where is Anna-Maria?" she asked, her tone was not nearly as even as mine.

Galt took a couple of steps forward and crouched down a bit like one might do when talking to a real four-year-old. "I'm sorry that your friend had to go. Poor girl scares easily."

There was laughter from his two sidekicks.

There is a dark side to being a ghost. Those bad movies Hollywood makes about ghosts are inspired by folks like Galt and his gang that mess with the living for spite and fun and can do a lot worse when they want to.

"You better not have hurt her," I said.

He stood up straight and took another step forward until we were nearly nose to nose. "Whatcha ya gonna do about it, Walter? Are you ready to 'destroy' me now?"

I had been mad the first time I had confronted Galt. The case with Haley had gotten complicated. I had formed feelings for the girl and Galt's pushing her toward the darker parts of the afterlife had caused her to cross lines, do things that couldn't be undone, which had destabilized her. In my anger, I had threatened to "destroy" him.

"Leave," I said.

"Why should we?" he asked, and his companions chuckled.

"Because if you don't," I said calmly, "I'm going to let Emily do to you guys what I made her promise to never do again."

Before I was a dentist, I was an actor. Played a couple of bit parts on TV shows in the late nineties. I had enough skill to sell it.

Emily chuckled next to me. It was half growl, and Galt stepped back and everyone was silent as the wind blew and the trees creaked and a few pine needles swirled around us. In the distance I could hear the traffic on 89A and the warbling of a siren coming this way.

What I said was something of a bluff, but I honestly didn't know how much. Emily, despite her appearances, was one of the most experienced ghosts around. She was formidable. Did she actually have the skills to hurt another ghost? I didn't know, but they didn't either.

Galt smiled a smug little smile and slowly nodded his head. "We'll move on... this time. There's nothing much to see here anyway. Just a dead guy. Boring." He took a few slow steps backwards.

"Where is Anna-Maria?" I asked.

He shrugged and when he got to his companions, he took their arms and they all popped away.

Chapter Nine

IT'S A SILLY THING, BUT FOR THE MOST PART I JUST WANT
to solve murders without interference and without an audi-
ence. With the ghosts I trust. With my friends.

We were a clique as were Galt and his goth boys. I
knew this. It's how societies form, living and dead.

But what we were doing was important. This time
more important than usual. I didn't even have to wonder
about how they knew about the murder. That graveyard
grapevine had done its job.

After they left, I turned to Emily and said, "I'll stay
here, you go pop to Anna-Maria."

That's the thing. A ghost like Emily can pop not only to
a location but to a person.

"I could have torn them up, you know," she said, her
voice a growl again.

"I know, honey," I said with a grim smile, trying to ban
the image of little Emily with her cute blond curls laying
into those boys like a rabid squirrel. It made me wonder
what paths her eighty-year afterlife had led her down, what
things she didn't talk about.

I had fought another ghost on the Hollywood case, but it felt like (and probably looked like) a couple of kids who didn't know what the hell they were doing. We aren't physical, we are energy, and I don't really know what a proper ghost fight is like, but that is probably a clue right there.

Our graveyard in Tucson is a congenial and peaceful place. I had only ever heard of one other fight, one JJ Lynch had gotten in with some ghosts in Globe, Arizona, something he wrote about in his first memoir.

I took a step forward to make sure that nothing had changed with the body when I realized that Emily was still here.

I turned and her face was squeezed in concentration. This wasn't right.

She looked at me, her eyes wide. "I can't... she's not..."

I looked around, not that that would help. I felt paranoid again. Had something happened to Anna-Maria?

"She's not what?" I asked, keeping my voice as calm as I could. The warble of the sirens was getting closer.

"She's not where I can find her," Emily said slowly.

I nodded. There were only two possibilities. She had answered the call and moved on, which seemed highly unlikely, or she had "faded."

Faded is what we call the state of an exhausted ghost. If you are in the presence of one while they are doing it, they quite literally fade away. We don't have unlimited energy, we need to rest, and if we don't rest for long enough, we have to fade.

And no one knows where we are when we fade. We are just gone. Completely. And when we come back, it's like waking up from the deepest sleep you can imagine. No dreams. No memories.

How long you are faded is also variable depending on how depleted you were.

An anger stirred in me and all I wanted to do was to destroy Galt. Anna-Maria was no pushover. When these ghosts had come here, she would have asked them to leave and wouldn't have taken no for an answer. She does not scare easily. Galt and his boys had done this.

I looked at Emily and saw the anger in her face. This had been a day so far. First a body and our conclusion that this corpse had been put here to get our attention. Emily and I not exactly getting along. And now Galt and his gang had messed with one of our own.

"Could they have hurt her? Permanently?" I asked.

She shook her head, but the movement was a bit too tentative for my liking. "Not physically," she said. "She'll be fine when she comes back, but…"

"But what?"

Her eyes narrowed and she studied my face with an intensity that made me want to turn and run. "Being a ghost is all a mental game. You know this. We all have unfinished business. If they pushed the right buttons, she might not be a-okay when she is done fading."

I nodded and bit my lip. The sirens were closer, but their approach had slowed. This was definitely about us. Tamara must have called it in, and the dirt roads were slowing down the emergency vehicles.

"There's going to be a reckoning when this is all over," Emily growled, and I knew she wasn't talking just about Galt and his boys.

Chapter Ten

WE WERE IN THE COUNTRY, SO IT WAS TWO SUVS FROM the sheriff's office that came first and secured the scene. The Flagstaff Police Department came next, and then the meat wagon from the county medical examiner.

The dark night was now lit up with harsh white lights and flashing blues and reds strobing against the tall pine trees.

This is what we wanted. This is what we needed. But it was a grim business and it took the rest of the night.

The scene was secured. The evidence was collected. Pictures were taken. And Emily and I were with them all of the way, seeing what they saw, remembering what they said.

They found the knife. They photographed the scuffed-up area where "Vince" and "Paul" had fought. They photographed the tire tracks on the dirt road, and finally they got to the body.

There were whispers and eyes a bit wider than they needed to be. Officers looking behind them more than they might have. This world was beginning to believe in ghosts, to believe in the afterlife, and they knew that ghosts had found this body.

The medical examiner was a woman of about forty with short brown hair and deep frown lines and dark circles under her eyes. She had on blue slacks and a green fleece jacket. She had her blue latex gloves on and was slowly examining the body. She reached into his back pockets, which were exposed and readily accessible.

"No ID," she said. A square-jawed young man with brown hair and a short beard behind her scribbled notes on a clipboard. He was also dressed in civilian clothing.

"Here's the needle site *they* mentioned," she said, shining a bright flashlight on Vince's right arm at the crease. There was something about the way she said "they." As if she was surprised to find the information good. "I... I concur, this was definitely an injection."

She went to his face which was turned to the right and pulled open one of his eyes. "Brown eyes, pupils dilated. Likely drugged. We'll need to check the blood to be sure."

Emily stepped closer and so did I. This was what we were waiting for. This was what we couldn't do.

"Now on to the cuts," she said with a sigh as she gently opened up a slice in his black T-shirt to examine one of them. "This one is about four inches long, but the cut is only a few millimeters deep." She dabbed at the spot with some gauze and gently opened it with her gloved fingers. "It went through the dermis and the hypodermis and into the muscle, but only barely. Whatever did this was extremely sharp and whoever did it was careful. With something this sharp they could have gone very deep. The cut is extremely straight and it looks like it was done quickly."

Could a sword or machete do a cut that controlled? I didn't think so. What the hell happened here?

The night dragged on and I was wishing that I could fade and just escape all of this, sink into blessed unconsciousness, have a few moments free from the horror of it all.

The medical examiner, her name was Wendy, and her assistant slowly cataloged all the wounds on the back of the body, some sixty-two of them, and then some sheriff's deputies helped them turn the body over.

It was the same on the front, sixty-two precise cuts that went through the skin and just into the muscle. On his legs, his torso, and his face. No single wound life-threatening, but all of them together turning into something mortal.

The T-shirt was a faded concert T-shirt of the Rolling Stones. That didn't seem to be a clue. The kid had no identification on him and nothing in his pockets. And that was strange too.

As the sun was just starting to lighten the eastern horizon in a gentle predawn glow, they zipped the corpse up into a body bag and loaded it into the back of the medical examiner's SUV.

All the living were moving around sluggishly despite the coffee many of them had been drinking. Eyes were too wide and conversations were quiet and stilted.

Flagstaff is a small town. You don't see this kind of thing around here. Hell, I hope that this is the kind of thing that no one sees anywhere.

"Should I go try to get help again?" Emily asked. We were standing on top of a sheriff's SUV just watching quietly. And we needed help. We needed someone to stay with the body while we tried to figure out where the arrow pointed.

I rolled it over. We had Galt and his goth ghosts likely to harass whoever volunteered, so we needed someone they were afraid of. "Yeah," I said with a smile. "See if you can get Banquo to help us."

Emily looked puzzled at first. I wasn't a big fan of Banquo's, for lots of reasons. He wasn't a bad guy, not at all, it was just… well, Emily had a huge crush on him and he was the leader of all the plays that were put on at the graveyard. It might be a bit—or a lot—petty, but that had kept me from really getting to know him. Oh, that and the fact that he was always in teacher mode and always pontificating, which got on my nerves.

And then Emily looked excited as the "crush" part of this kicked in. I was glad to see a glimmer of something besides angst and worry and disgust.

"We need a ghost Galt won't mess with," I said. "Now, go."

With a pop she was gone, and I flew up and watched the scene from a few hundred feet up, which helped. The living looked much smaller which gave the illusion that the challenge we were facing was just a bit smaller too.

It was a trick, I know, but right then I needed anything I could get.

Chapter Eleven

"THANK YOU FOR HELPING," I SAID TO BANQUO AFTER they popped back. We were all hovering over the scene, the meat wagon was just pulling out slowly over the rocky land, and the horizon had lightened just a touch.

Banquo was older, looking to be in his sixties, with a bald head and a thin strip of grey hair. He was short with a large belly and his form was very crisp and barely transparent. He wore dark slacks and a long-sleeve button-down shirt.

"Of course, my boy," Banquo said with a grim smile, his voice deep and resonant. "'Desperate times breed desperate measures,' as the bard said."

Banquo was always quoting Shakespeare. That was another thing I wasn't fond of. I mean, Shakespeare and his plays are amazing, but as a modern actor, I would prefer some more modern plays. How about a nice Sam Shepard play? Maybe "Fool for Love."

But in this case, I loved the quote. Not because it was accurate, which it very much was, but because it was Banquo making a subtle dig at me, saying that I must be desperate if I had wanted his help. Which meant that maybe I annoyed him some too, and…

Yeah, yeah, I know. It was a petty line of thinking and it wouldn't seem like we had time for subtle jabs, but it was honestly just what I needed. Knowing that Banquo was maybe a bit jealous of me and my friendship with Emily was like a shot of espresso waking me up.

"Indeed," I said to Banquo. "We need all the help we can get on this one."

"Then I best be to it," he said, flying down to the meat wagon.

"What now?" Emily asked, her eyes a bit wide and on Banquo. I honestly didn't know if Banquo was unaware of the crush or just ignoring it. Whatever the case was, this was yet another thing I didn't like about him. Emily deserved better.

I gave her a grim smile and said, "Now, we follow the arrow."

Below us the dark red stain where the body had been was still on the ground and still clearly marked the direction.

———

A SINGLE ARROW SUCKS AS A CLUE. WE WERE ASSUMING that it indicated direction, that it was precisely placed by the murderer. And even if we assumed they had GPS and a great compass, it was executed by a dying man crawling over the forest floor and couldn't be 100 percent accurate.

This was the very definition of a long shot.

Just the kind of thing Emily and I tended to take on.

And I would have been happy—well, let's be honest, and say less grumpy—to explore it as the sun came up over

48

the mountain town and the clouds started to break from the storm that didn't quite materialize last night.

But it wasn't that simple. Our working theory was that this young man had been murdered to get our attention, and that changed everything.

But we worked it, nevertheless.

Emily stayed behind the arrow and acted as spotter as I flew forward. She had discarded the need to be carried. There was no getting around flying for this. I flew out slowly and she guided my path with small adjustments until I had a landmark to follow, which were towers on the east side of Mount Elden.

Elden is the low, rocky mountain that hangs over the east part of Flagstaff. It rises about 2,300 feet from the surrounding town and is covered in ponderosa pine trees, except for the eastern portion which had a devastating forest fire in the seventies that land is still recovering from. There are towers on that side of the mountain and that seemed to be just about perfect.

I flew slowly and listened carefully as Emily guided me.

She used her fine popping abilities and would pop from the arrow, close enough for me to hear her, and adjust my course if needed, and then she would pop back.

We were high enough so there was a clear line of sight, and ghostly vision being free of biology is pretty fantastic so she could see me from a long ways away.

My path took me first over 89A, a two-lane road that cut through the thick forest. Then over the golf courses and large homes of the gated community called Forest Highlands. Then over a working-class community called Kachina Village. Then over I-17, a divided highway running north/south, then the Flagstaff Airport, some more homes, and finally to twirling on-ramps and off-ramps where the east/west I-40 met the I-17.

I made sure I had my landmark fixed and stopped.

This had taken a good hour. We went slowly. We looked for anything below us that might stand out over the entire way. But there was already too much ground to cover, too much to search. And as soon as we crossed the highways we would be into the university and the main part of Flagstaff.

"This is useless," I said when Emily noticed I had stopped and popped to me.

She nodded, her green eyes looking a shade darker than usual. "We're missing something."

I nodded. "We have to be. Either the arrow isn't the clue we thought it was or we don't have enough information. The arrow gives us a direction, not a distance."

Emily shrugged. "So we search all of Flagstaff."

I nodded. "Looking for what? A sign that says, 'I am the red arrow murderer, come arrest me, you damn clever ghosts'?"

Emily pursed her lips and narrowed her eyes. She and I had unfinished business and my grumpiness level was going up and no one was having any fun.

"Sorry," I said. "I'm… I'm just a bit freaked out about this."

She nodded. "Pretend you're not having a little fit, what would you do?"

Ouch. I sighed and let the "little fit" part go. I took some deep breaths and tried to calm my mind. As I've explained before, ghosts most definitely do not breathe, but the more we act like the living the more we feel like the living, so those "deep breaths" have an analogous effect on ghosts.

I stared at the traffic whirling below us. Even though it was early there were cars on the road and even more semis. I-40 runs nearly the entire width of the country.

The patterns were lulling, the drone of the engines and the hum of the tires soothed my stressed mind as I "breathed."

So we had direction not distance. We had a body around here somewhere with the medical examiner working on it and Banquo watching them. We had a murder that was theoretically done to get our attention. And if the murderer wanted to get our attention, they wouldn't just give us one clue and then leave us hanging.

The murderer was playing a game with us. A sick game, but a game nevertheless.

"Sixty-two," I said slowly. "The victim had sixty-two cuts on his front and his back."

"And that has to be on purpose," Emily said with a wicked smile, her green eyes sparking.

I nodded. "One hundred twenty-four in total."

"So is that distance?" she asked, "to go along with direction?"

"Maybe, but are we talking meters, kilometers, or miles?" I asked. "And was it sixty-two on both sides to get our attention or to make up 124?"

"And we're ghosts," Emily said. "Sure, we can follow a direction, but we can't measure distance accurately."

"So what then?" I asked. "A house number? A street address?"

"Maybe," Emily said, and her cheerful expression let me know that while we had our unfinished business to deal with, she was back on the case. "Let's fly back. You stay up high and I'll search for sixty-two or 124 below."

I nodded. It was a long shot, but at least we had a theory and a plan.

Emily's grim smile melted from her face and her eyes defocused and she swiveled in the air and looked to the southeast.

I didn't say anything. I knew better. She wasn't alive, so it wasn't like she was having a stroke or something. I had only seen her do this a couple of times, but I knew what it was. It was her murder radar, or whatever you want to call it. Someone else had died.

"Oh, no," she said, her eyes wide and focusing on me.

"What?"

"There's been another murder," she said slowly, her smooth forehead furrowing. "Walter, I think we have a serial killer on our hands."

Chapter Twelve

WHEN YOU THINK OF FLAGSTAFF, YOU THINK OF THE
forest. The tall ponderosa pine trees with their brown bark
and their dark green needles in bundles of three. They are
everywhere. The early settlers came to harvest the trees
and had to beat them back to make room for humans.

When Emily popped us to the murder she had just
sensed, we were back in the forest in another area where
the density of trees was relatively low and the rocky ground
was covered in dried, tawny pine needles with a scattering
of pinecones. Another body lay on the ground, a streak of
dark red blood behind it.

"Shit!" I said.

We were sooner this time. The body still had spots of
red blood while the tail of the arrow was a dark ochre red.
It was a young woman, the ends of her long blond hair
thick with blood and sticking to the sweatshirt she was
wearing. She had tights and running shoes. And she had
precise cut after cut all over her body. She was lying facedown and the arms were arranged to turn her into a
perfect arrow. She was pointed north-ish.

I grabbed Emily and flew us up high and fast. I needed to know where we were. I needed to see if we could spot a vehicle moving away. I needed to get away from that corpse.

I cursed as I flew us, and Emily didn't even say a word, didn't tell me to mind my language, didn't tell me to get my "mitts" off of her.

Solving a murder once it's done can certainly be stressful. Solving murders that are being committed because of you, was a whole different thing.

"This is about us," I said between curses.

"No shit, Sherlock," Emily growled. I don't think I had ever heard her curse. This was serious.

The body was in the forest east of I-17 and south of town. There were dirt roads ambling around it, but none close and no trails. To the east was Lake Mary Road which headed out southeast from Flagstaff.

The terrain was flatter, but otherwise the same as where we found the other body.

Except this one pointed almost due north towards Northern Arizona University (NAU). Just like the other arrow. We had found our missing clue.

There were two arrows and together they pointed to a single spot.

Dammit!

"No cars," I muttered, studying the dirt roads.

"Don't bother," Emily said. "Our perp has medical training. They left themselves enough time to get away before the victim died. Before I would notice."

She was right. Shit!

I nodded. "The precise cuts reinforce that assessment," I said. "I'm beginning to think the murder weapon is a scalpel."

I flew us back down to the body and sure enough there

was a small puncture in the fold of the right arm.

"So the perp drugs the victims," I said, pointing out the needle mark, "slices them up, and coaxes them to crawl in a line as they bleed."

"And then is long gone before they actually die," Emily added.

"And no ghost," I said. "Not with either of them. A ghost could ID the murderer."

Emily glanced down at the body. "Too soon to tell."

I shook my head. I knew there wouldn't be a ghost, that the murderer had chosen carefully to find people that weren't full of regret. Had used drugs to mask the trauma of their passage. This was part of their plan too.

Although the sun was crawling above the horizon and the day was lightening, I felt a darkness bearing down on me. Despite being in the forest, I felt claustrophobic like the trees were closing in.

These murders were my fault.

If I hadn't been writing about these cases, about Emily and her ability to sense murders, these people would still be alive. And yeah, I get that I wasn't the sicko murderer, but my writing, my therapy, had been used to fuel these acts. Even if you are being charitable it's clear that I am the catalyst in all of this.

Me. Thinking I was so clever to catch these murderers. Going to the SECI chamber and writing about my life to help me come to terms with it.

I had done this.

"…what do you think, Walter?" Emily was saying, her voice sounding distant.

I felt the need to escape more strongly than I had since I was alive. Since I kicked my gambling addiction, since I stopped shooting myself up with propofol from my dental practice, since right before Emily found me when I was haunting my office manager and out of clues.

I was staring at the body. The woman was thin and from what I could see of her face, maybe twenty years old. She wasn't some washed-up actor with a failed marriage and a career he liked but didn't love. She wasn't depressed and lonely and desperate. She had her whole life in front of her, at least until I came along.

"Walter!" Emily was shouting now and I could hear the urgency in her voice but I couldn't pay attention to her. I could only stare at the girl and watch the blood slowly dry.

Part of me knew what was happening. I was sinking into that ghostly state that we call the bardo. A place where you are trapped by your regrets. All those wispy moaning ghosts that are a part of how the living view the dead, those ghosts are in the bardo, trapped in their own hell, unable to escape their regrets.

And the part of me that knew I was sinking into the bardo knew without a doubt that I deserved to be there.

I had failed at acting, the thing that I had loved so.

I had failed my wife and our unborn child and watched my marriage crumble.

I had failed to create a life worth living in Tucson.

And I had failed to know that someone wanted to murder me and let them use my known propofol addiction against me. I had died in one of my dental chairs, the needle still in my arm, the milky white bottle of propofol close by. My death had been ruled a suicide.

And I had new leads on who killed me and I screwed that up too. I hadn't told Emily and I had let that killer get away with it.

I wasn't even a very good detective.

I deserved to be in the Bardo.

"Walter!" Emily screamed as she slapped my face.

It wasn't just that numb, barely there ghostly touch. What Emily did to me was something different. She put her energy and her intent into it. She flew up so our heads were even and let me have it.

I felt an electric shock flow through me and the darkness that had almost swallowed me receded a bit.

She slapped me again.

"But… this is… I…" I mumbled.

Another slap.

I had heard of several techniques for helping a ghost slipping into the bardo, and none of them ever involved slapping. Leave it to Emily.

"You don't get to do this, Walter," she said, hysteria edging into her voice. "You don't get to leave me. Not you." She slapped me again, harder, a zap of energy flowing through my body akin to rubbing your feet on the carpet and touching something metal.

For a ghost it was an extreme sensation.

She slapped me again and again, but I didn't want to come back. I had screwed up my life and I had screwed up my afterlife. Emily was still talking, but I wasn't listening to her, the darkness coming back despite the energy she was pumping into me.

And then I could hear it, the bardo. It was calling to me, not using words, but something deeper and more primal. It was promising me relief from all of my suffering, an end to all this running around and trying to solve murders or the painful process of closure with my ex-wife, and an end to all the loneliness.

It was sweet and insistent, the call of the bardo, but not pure. It wasn't sound or taste or any particular sense, more like the irresistible tug of gravity. I was going, nothing could stop me. The bardo just had to be better than this afterlife.

Part of me knew that was a lie. That the bardo wasn't about escaping your mistakes but endlessly reliving the worst of them. The bardo played the same music and held the same promise as my addictions had. It was like the gambling and the propofol, promising escape but actually making things worse, much worse. But the part of me that knew that wasn't in control.

The forest darkened further like the darkest of nights and I was almost gone when I heard crying.

Not the quiet tears of an adult but the desperate wailing of a child, hurt and inconsolable. The unfettered crying of youth before they started bottling up their emotions to be an adult.

It was louder than the call of the bardo and it pulled at my heart.

And then I knew who was crying. Emily. It was the kind of crying that leaves your eyes red-rimmed and snot running down your face. It was the cry of a child that had lost what it cared about the most.

And even I, with all my self-loathing, could not let that be. I had to go to that cry. I had to help.

It took every ounce of will I had, but I turned from the bardo and towards the crying child, towards Emily.

The world came back to me and I took her in my arms as she wailed. "I've got you, honey," I said. "I won't leave you. I promise I won't leave you."

Emily's crying slowed until she was making less noise but her chest was still heaving with emotion. "Don't... don't make promises you... you can't keep, Walter," she managed to get out and then the wailing took her again.

And this was part of what was between us that we didn't talk about.

I had been trying to move on from this afterlife since I got here. The bardo wasn't the right way, I knew that now that I was rational again, but there was something beyond this life as an earth-bound spirit and I was determined to get there. As soon as I solved my own murder. Which I had enough information to go try to do now.

I held her as tightly as I could and gently rocked her there in the early morning in the forest south of Flagstaff next to our serial killer's bloody second victim.

"I won't leave you, Emily," I said, my voice thick with emotion. "Not until we catch the bastard that did this."

Chapter Thirteen

EMILY CAME BACK TO HERSELF FAIRLY QUICKLY, WIPED the snot off her face and said, "Get your hands off me, you perv." But there wasn't much energy behind it and her eyes remained red rimmed, although as a ghost there was no reason for that.

I put her down.

"We need help," I said, slowly. I was ashamed. I knew we needed to talk more, but the corpse and trail of blood laid out like a red arrow had to be the priority. There would be time enough for all that shame and all that talking later.

She nodded.

"I know where we are well enough to describe it," I said. "Can you pop me to the SECI chamber so we can get the authorities out here?"

She nodded again, wiping more snot off her face.

"And then you need to find someone to stay with the body while we go follow the arrows."

"Who?" she asked. "Fredrick was making excuses last night and Blinky faded to avoid me, and Anna-Maria..."

She trailed off. Anna-Maria was an issue, but we had more pressing ones. I bit my lip and nodded, hoping Anna-Maria was just faded. I racked my brain. We needed someone fearless, someone who wouldn't care that the living were stalking the dead. No. We needed someone who would be pissed that the living were stalking the dead.

"JJ," I said. "We need JJ."

JJ Lynch knew Tamara and Jin when he was alive. He helped them build the first SECI chamber and was the first ghost to use it. He had written two long memoirs in it and once entered the bardo of his own free will to rescue someone he didn't know.

"He ain't afraid of no living," Emily said, a smile cracking through her grief like the sun lancing through the clouds after a violent storm.

"Think he'll help?" I asked.

Emily smiled coyly. "Oh… I think he likes me."

I laughed, it was strained and short lived, but I was grateful for it.

"Good," I said. "We have a plan. But before we go, we need to do some counting." I took a deep breath and looked at the body and all the cuts through the clothing and into the skin.

Emily's jaw set and she nodded and we got down to it.

JJ FOR ALL HIS DARING DO, IS A KIND AND GENTLE BEING. He's medium height and medium build with brown hair buzzed short and intense blue-grey eyes. He looked to be about thirty years old and was dressed simply in jeans and a long-sleeved black T-shirt.

As soon as I was done at the SECI chamber, Emily was

there with JJ and she popped us all back to the forest. She was showing him the body and all that we had found.

"And here is the injection sight," she said, pointing at the needle mark on the right arm. "We believe some kind of drug was used to make the victim docile."

JJ nodded, looking closely where she pointed.

"She has sixty-two cuts on her back, just like the last victim," Emily continued. "And if our perp is true to form, there will be sixty-two cuts on her front."

"Why would they do that?" JJ asked.

Emily shrugged her tiny shoulders. "We haven't figured that out, but we think it's a clue."

Emily went on walking JJ through what we had found, but I wasn't listening. He had said, "Why would *they* do that." They. I'm sure he just chose a gender-neutral pronoun and English being bad at that had chosen "they." But what if earlier when I had chosen to call the perpetrator "Paul" I had biased my thinking in two ways. In thinking a man did it and thinking a single person did it.

We had no evidence of either.

Emily was done and they were both looking at me, so I shook it off. "I really appreciate this, JJ," I said.

He gave me a short nod.

"I would expect Galt and his boys to show up," I added. "Not sure why, but they seem to be interested in this one."

JJ shrugged.

"They messed with Anna-Maria," Emily said with a bit of a growl.

He smiled at the girl and shrugged casually again. "They show up," he said, "I will nicely ask them to leave. They don't leave, maybe they're ready to answer the call."

Emily blinked, her jaw wide and I could see her crush get that much more crushing. There was the paradoxical combination of humility and confidence to him and apparently Emily couldn't get enough of it.

Some ghosts have specialties. Emily can pop. Blinky, the absent member of our team, specializes in looking like inanimate objects—which is quite tricky to do with the "more you act like the living the better you feel" thing. And JJ, he can summon the call… and not say yes to it, somehow.

I've never experienced the call, but I hear it is like hearing the most beautiful music that you just can't describe. Unlike how the bardo calls to you, "the call" is full of nurturing energy and the promise of a better existence. It is the reward I have been striving toward, the reason I turned myself into a detective, it is my escape from this existence as an earth-bound spirit.

It's a one-way trip, so we don't know what's on the other side of the call. Except as ghosts we know for sure that there is an afterlife so there must be something there when you "move on."

It was only a moment, my mind churned through all of that and I found myself looking into JJ's kind eyes. "Umm… Can you… I…" I stammered looking a lot sillier than Emily with her crush. I took a deep breath. "I might need your help," I said. "After this is all over."

His eyes widened as he comprehended what I was saying. "That would be my honor, Walter."

I stood there for a moment more, my eyes locked with JJ's. I just couldn't look away. JJ, being Banquo's apprentice, wasn't someone I had spent a lot of time with and I was regretting that. I was regretting my jealousy towards Banquo too.

"Thank you," I finally said, looking at Emily who was staring at me. "We better get going."

JJ smiled. "You guys are so brave. Go find who did this. Stop these murders. I got this."

I picked Emily up and floated us up several hundred feet so we could orient on this arrow.

"You've got a crush on JJ Lynch," Emily hissed in my ear.

"I do not," I said. "You have the crush."

Her cheeks flushed red and she said loudly, "I do not, you do."

"I do not," I said. "I am heterosexual."

She snorted. "As if that matters anymore, it's not like you have a ding-dong or anything."

"Emily!"

The embarrassing part of all this was, that ghostly hearing being as good as it is, JJ probably heard every damn word.

Chapter Fourteen

IT TOOK TIME. FOR EMILY AND ME TO GET BACK INTO the game after my brush with the bardo and our time with JJ. For us to get oriented on this bloody arrow and for me to fly forward with Emily spotting like with the last arrow. And more time to go back and redo that arrow.

We checked and double-checked. We triangulated. We stayed focused and we ended up floating above a large building on the south campus of NAU.

The building was comprised of two large square sections, the bottom right edge of one almost touching the top left corner of the other. Bridging the two was a third square section offset at 45 degrees and joining the other two.

The main square sections had pitched roofs that peaked in the center of the building making them look like two large Xs from above.

I cursed.

A lot.

I knew this was the spot. The murderer was playing with us and knowing the arrows would be a bit imprecise, the goddamn location for us to find was marked by huge Xs.

Emily just stared at me, her face gone pale. I was holding her on my hip since we were together and she preferred not to fly.

"Well…" I began, not really having words for any of this.

"Oh boy," Emily sighed. "What have we gotten…? Oh boy."

Fear doesn't leave you when you're dead, not at all. But the fear of someone hurting you physically does because you are not physical anymore. But what I was feeling hovering over those two giant Xs was that kind of fear. Like someone was out to hurt me and it was personal.

"We… we should go search," I said, remembering how JJ had just called us brave and feeling anything but.

"Yes, we should," Emily said, her voice eerily calm.

We just hovered there.

A minute ticked by and we both just stared.

"I'm sorry," I finally said.

Emily's green eyes found mine. "What for?"

I sighed. "For not telling you right away about the clues I found when I wrote about my last days. For typing all these cases up and fueling the madness of the psycho that did this. For being a general grump and not being nearly good enough for you, Em."

Her eyes widened and she stared at me for a moment, and then floating above NAU, she pulled me into a fierce hug. "I love you too, Walter," she whispered with a sniff.

And then I was crying. God, how many emotions can I have in one damn day?

I do love Emily. Not in the crushing way of romance but in a deeply unique way. It was like she was both my mother and my daughter at the same time. I loved her as the person that saved my afterlife and as my best dead friend.

There were tears on her face when the hug ended. "One more case after this one, Walter," she said slowly. "And then you can move on." Her face clouded and the slow trickle of tears threatened to turn into a raging river, but she sniffed and her face hardened. "You should move on if you want to. Don't you dare stay for me."

I nodded.

"Do you hear me?" she said, loudly this time, pushing away from me and floating on her own there up in the air. "I don't need you to stay for me." Her nostrils flared and she put her little fists on her hips.

My own tears threatened torrential proportions and all I could do was nod, and I loved this strange tough little ghost all that much more.

"Now let's do this," she said her lip curling comically in a four-year-old's version of defiance.

I nodded and we both started flying down when there was a pop and Banquo was there.

His round face was white and his grey eyes were wide. "Wait," he said. "There's something you have to know."

Chapter Fifteen

I DIED OF AN OVERDOSE OF PROPOFOL. THE DRUG IS AN anesthetic, a tricky one to administer, and an easy one to overdose on. It doesn't really take pain away, but it leaves you just not caring about the pain. It allows you to disconnect from it in this most amazing way.

It can also wipe your short-term memory, which can be quite useful sometimes.

Propofol is not as regulated as some other drugs and not that hard to get, especially if you are running a dental practice.

I loved propofol. I knew my problems weren't gone, but when I was high on it, I could float along in a cloud of "I just don't care." It was the relief I craved, but it wasn't earned. It wasn't real.

And I hate propofol, because I wasted all that time with it and it ended my life.

My afterlife was built on the foundation of "I was murdered." It gave me purpose. It gave me ambition. It gave me my unfinished business.

When I was writing the story of how I died, I was

forced to confront the fact that since I have no memory of it, that I might have done it myself. I might have over-dosed, although Emily insists that she can smell murder and I stink of it (this despite the fact that ghosts have no sense of smell).

I tell you all this so you'll understand how what Banquo said hit me.

He popped in looking half-terrified, and let me tell you, this is not Banquo's normal demeanor. He's the rock of the graveyard, the one who is always helping other ghosts.

"Propofol," he said with a gasp. "They found propofol in the victim's blood."

Before I had believed these murders were about me. Now I knew.

I couldn't hear the sound of the cars on the highway just to our south or the birds greeting the fall morning anymore. The darkness of the bardo was calling again, but I paid it no mind. I felt a rage spark deep in me and I wanted to hurt someone. Badly. I wanted to find who did this and yank them across the veil, make them a ghost, and then I wanted to take my ghostly hands and figure out how to beat them senseless.

This was more than personal on the part of the murderer (or murderers). This was cruelness at a level I don't think I had ever experienced.

It was fight or flight time again, and unlike before when I was falling towards the flight of the bardo, I wanted to fight. I was ready to fight. I needed to fight.

"Thank you," I said to Banquo, my voice sounding strangely calm and oddly distant. "Did they find anything else or just propofol?"

Banquo's eyes narrowed and his focus seemed like he was looking through me. Into me. "They think there may be more," he said, "but they haven't identified them yet."

I nodded. Emily was right, we needed to solve this case. That was the only thing that mattered. We needed to stop whoever was doing this.

"Are you okay, Walter?" Banquo asked.

I smiled. I know it looked stiff and weird, but it was the best I could manage. "I will be once we solve this case." I turned to Emily. "Are you ready?"

She was staring at me too. They both knew my past, they must have had a clue how this hit me. I think they were expecting more of a reaction.

And I was having one, but I was keeping it inside, letting the fire slowly grow, waiting for when I could unleash it.

I didn't wait, I flew down to the huge two Xs to find the next clue the killer had left us.

Chapter Sixteen

THE BUILDING WAS A STUDENT UNION CALLED THE DU Bois Center. I think it used to be two separate buildings and they built the diagonal piece to join the two large squares. It had tiled floors and comfortable sitting areas and places to eat. It had a ballroom and conference rooms, and this early in the morning there was only a janitor there mopping the floor.

It didn't take long to find the clue, and when I did the spark inside of me threatened to go nuclear.

Along one of the winding hallways on the main level there was a desk that said "NAU Box Office." They sold tickets to events on campus. On the wall were two glassed-in frames that held posters of upcoming events.

The first poster was of an upcoming production of "A Midsummer Night's Dream." More Shakespeare. I almost groaned.

The next poster wasn't right. It took a moment for it to register it was so not right. My mind slipped a gear. I recognized it, of course. I used to have this same poster hanging in my living room as a form of torture, as a reminder of the past that I had lost.

Central to the poster was a beautiful woman of Korean descent standing at an angle to the camera, her head turned to face it. She had high cheekbones and was Hollywood beautiful with full lips and a perfectly symmetrical face. She wore a dark blue pantsuit and her long, silky black hair was pulled back into a ponytail. On her hip was clipped a brass police badge.

To her left and right, fading into the distance where four other figures, three men and another woman, all of them standing up straight, some with their arms crossed. They were all standing on aged and cracked blacktop and in the background was the Los Angeles skyline.

The top read "Detectives: LA — coming fall of 2010." And right below it "Season Five."

This was no NAU event. Someone had put that there for me to find. That woman was Sun Parker. My ex-wife. The love of my life. For season five of the show they made what they called "hero" posters with each one of the five leads taking the center for one of them.

This was Sun's hero poster.

Sun's huge success and this series had come a while after our divorce. I had looked at that poster every day after I had gotten it. They were promotional only, not for sale, but I still had plenty of Hollywood friends.

I loved that poster and I hated that poster.

On one hand, I was so proud of Sun, she had made it. On the other hand, it was a reminder of what I had and what I lost. I am not Hollywood beautiful, more character actor material, and somehow I had ended up with that amazing woman. We had been in love. For real. I've already written about all of this, so I won't repeat myself here, but suffice it to say if the killer wanted to sucker punch me, this was the perfect thing.

"Walter...?" Emily gasped when she saw the poster. "That's... it's..."

I nodded. I couldn't speak. I felt like the wind had been knocked out of me.

"Is this the clue?" Emily asked.

"Yes," I said, before even thinking about it. "The killer used propofol on their victims." My voice was droning and flat. "The red arrows pointed to the X. The X holds a poster of Sun. The killer has pointed us at Sun and took two lives doing it."

Emily gasped, her hand flying to her mouth. "I... we... Oh, God," she mumbled.

If not for the spark, if not for that seed of anger, I think the bardo would have taken me. It called to me of escape, but I understood how it lied. The same way propofol lied to me, except the bardo never let you forget, not for a moment.

The killer wanted to hurt me, as badly as possible. Sun was the way to do that, especially now that we had had some closure and healing.

The spark exploded in me and I felt a rage like I had never felt before. I had once promised to destroy Galt, but now I knew I would destroy whoever did this. I would do whatever it took. I would pay any price.

"Take me to Sun," I said, still staring at the poster and not looking at Emily.

The red arrows had just been the first act. The search was the second act. Now it was time for the climax, for the killer's third act, and I was determined that it would not end well for them.

"Walter, I don't think we should..."

"Take. Me. To. Sun." I said the words slowly, keeping

my tone even. I didn't want to scream at Emily, but it was taking everything I had not to.

I turned and met her eyes and she took a step back. "No, Walter. Not when you're like this."

Haley was like this when she found her killer, she was a fury right out of Greek mythology. She attached herself to her killer and did everything in her power to destroy him. And she was a brand-new ghost that was just operating on instinct. I had been this way a while. I knew I could do better. If I was willing to lose myself while doing it.

"Fine," I said and turned back to the poster focusing on the image of Sun, on her lovely brown eyes, making her my entire world like she once was when I was alive and young.

I knew the theory behind popping. You had to visualize something so strongly that it became real and then you were there with it.

I had popped once before, during the ghost bride case, because I needed to see Sun. I did then because I was desperate. I was desperate now.

I stared at her face on the poster. Sun's face I knew better than my own. This poster was a few years old so there were a few more delicate lines around her eyes and her smile lines were a tad deeper, but she was still the luminous beauty she always was.

And I had this fire burning in me and I had a mission, I had a purpose, and that brought me focus.

I made her my world until with a "pop" I was with her.

Chapter Seventeen

When I popped to her, Sun's beauty was present, but it was diminished by her left eye being swollen halfway shut, the bruising around it an angry red edging towards purple. Her hair was a bit disheveled and she wore jeans, hiking boots, and a flannel shirt. There was a rip in her jeans, a bloody wound underneath. The left shoulder of her shirt was ripped showing the strap of her black bra.

Someone had hurt her. That someone would pay.

I looked around and did a double take. I was in a small travel trailer while Sun sat on a couch, a steaming cup of tea on the small glass table next to her. She was focused on her phone, flipping casually. She didn't appear to be in distress although she looked tired.

Next to her was a script flipped open and some lines highlighted in yellow.

Wait a minute.

I got close and could see the artifice behind the damaged eye. Makeup. She was on set. If I had a heart, I think it would have beaten its way out of my chest by then.

Being on set has this feel to it. I did it more as a grip,

which has a very different vibe, but I did it enough as an actor to know the rhythm.

Long days and sometimes nights. Lots of waiting for the setups. And then you are on, so on, and have to throw everything you have into the scene.

It runs hot and cold. But when it's hot, it's scalding hot. It's everything you've got. It's whipsawed emotions and bright lights and dozens of crew staring at you and money being spent by the minute so you have to get it right.

It's adrenalized and high stakes when you are on, and I loved it.

It's boring and tedious when you're not, and you have to structure your day so you don't go mad. You can study lines, rehearse, take care of business, or just goof off. But you best have a plan to get through the psychotic nature of a day on set.

Or night.

It was early morning and the fatigue written on her face despite the makeup she wore was probably from shooting all night. I took a moment and flew through the trailer. It was just her. I looked out the window and saw tall green-needled pine trees.

She was fine. She was working. Thank God.

But she could easily be in Flagstaff and that worried me.

With a "pop," Emily appeared, her eyes going wide and her mouth opening when she saw Sun.

"It's makeup," I said, trying to keep my voice calm. "I think she just did a night shoot."

Emily looked at me and her brow furrowed as her eyes took me in. "Are you okay, Walter?"

"No!" I said, my voice loud. "I am most definitely not okay. I am furious. Look at those trees. We are probably still in the Flagstaff area. This is so not over. If something happens to Sun, I'll—"

My words were choked off by a knock on the door. My anger had twisted into fear by seeing what looked like a beaten Sun, even though I knew it wasn't real.

Sun put her phone down and stifled a yawn. It was still early, but honestly since I became a ghost it was hard for me to judge the time. It was somewhere around 7 a.m.

I looked around, my head snapping back and forth. I had forgotten something. I just knew it. I should have done more than just stare at Sun when I got here. She wasn't safe. I wasn't doing what needed to be done. I wasn't protecting her.

Sun opened the door, a smile lighting up her face, and suddenly she didn't look tired anymore. "You must be Mary," Sun said, stepping aside and letting another woman walk in.

A woman I knew.

A woman I knew well.

Mary Paulson used to be my dental assistant. My first hire when I started the dental practice. She was a big woman with brown eyes and round cheeks. Her blond hair was cut shorter than when I had seen her last, something of a pixie cut, and she looked older. A lot older.

It wasn't anything specific. She would be in her mid-thirties now, but the dark circles under her eyes and her slightly sallow complexion made her look older. The Mary I knew was a woman that smiled a lot and had the smile lines to prove it. On this older woman they looked like frown lines.

After going to the SECI chamber and writing about my death by propofol, I had remembered that Mary had a crush on me and I had never seen it. I had known that her marriage was troubled, that she was hoping her unplanned pregnancy would bring her and her husband closer. She had confided in me a lot. We had been friends, but I had never imagined anything else.

She had.

She was an army medic in Afghanistan before training to be a dental assistant. She knew all about propofol and the secret I hadn't told Emily was that I suspected she was involved in my murder.

I had played the scenarios out in my mind. Mary telling her husband about her feelings for me just after their baby had come. Him sneaking into the practice, confronting me, and overpowering me and shooting me up with propofol.

But that didn't work. He was a construction worker and before that a soldier. He wouldn't have the knowledge of propofol or the skill with a needle. There would have been a fight and my body showed no signs of one.

That left me with Mary as my murderer. She knew my problems with the drug, everyone in the office did, and knew exactly how to use a needle. But I couldn't face it.

Being dead and reflecting on my life, especially when I went back and relived my last day and my haunting of my dental practice, had slowly eroded my view of the life I had lived. The hindsight of a ghost, with our spectacular memories, changed it. Withered it. Left me with my mistakes and my grief and made my life something I didn't quite recognize.

You might be thinking that this is the work of an earth-bound spirit. To look at their lives and finish up their unfinished business. And it is. But it can be so very hard.

When I found the Mary clue, I turned away from it. I just couldn't handle it. She was my colleague and friend. Someone I worked with and relied on. Someone I confided in. If she was the one that killed me, that would erode the view of my life even further. Too far.

I just couldn't face it. So I avoided it. Refused to believe it.

But as I saw her standing awkwardly just inside the trailer, brushing at her short blond hair, her down jacket still on, I knew that I had been a fool.

I had been afraid to see it.

I had been unable to accept it.

Mary was my killer.

Mary was the red arrow murderer.

Mary was here to kill Sun.

Chapter Eighteen

I COULDN'T MOVE. I COULD HARDLY THINK. AND thankfully I didn't need to breathe. Emily had taken a hold of my arm, like she didn't want me to be able slip away again. She was looking at the two women, a puzzled look on her face.

"Don't worry about the eye," Sun said with a chuckle. "It's just makeup."

"Thank you for seeing me," Mary said, looking down and not meeting Sun's eyes. Mary was wearing jeans and a blue down jacket zipped all the way up. It was early fall and the mornings get cold, but it seemed like she was over-dressed.

"Of course," Sun said motioning towards the couch. "Would you like to sit? Can I get you some tea? I'm afraid I can't keep coffee around anymore… I used to drink way too much of it."

Mary looked up, smiled briefly and shook her head. "I'm okay. And I… I think I need to stand. I'm just so nervous." She shifted a large brown purse that was on her shoulder.

"That's fine," Sun said, grabbing her tea and taking a sip, but staying standing. "So, you worked for Walter?"

Mary nodded. "I… I feel so bad about what happened to him and I…" She took a deep breath. "Do you mind if we talk about something different? Just until… you know… I…" She brushed at her hair again with her left hand and I noticed she wasn't wearing a wedding ring anymore and wondered if that was part of the reason behind all of this.

Sun smiled and nodded. "Sure. What did you have in mind?"

She looked around, eyeing the trees just out the window. "What are you guys doing in Flagstaff? I thought your show took place in LA."

Emily looked at me, her eyes wide as she chewed on her lower lip. "It's her…? From your practice?" she whispered, even though the living couldn't hear us.

I just nodded.

"Oh, it does," Sun said. "This is the climax of a long storyline my character, Melissa Lee, is part of. Abusive relationship." She pointed at her eye. "But don't worry, the bastard gets his own in the end."

"Really?" Mary asked, suddenly seeming more normal. "Melissa Lee is such a confident, strong woman, how did she get caught up in this kind of thing?"

"The usual way these things happen," Sun said. "One small step at a time. One tiny abuse after another until…" she shrugged her shoulders.

"Have you…?" Mary asked, her eyes down again, but I could hear something hopeful in her tone.

"Me?" Sun asked, shaking her head. "No. Walter is a good man and I was lucky before him and I've been very careful since. But… I know women. We all know women." She was eying Mary, she caught it too. Mary had been abused in some way.

I remember Mary telling me of fights she and her husband would have where they would shout at each other, but she never mentioned anything physical and she never came to work with any visible wounds.

Mary nodded, her brow furrowed. "You said 'is.'"

"Excuse me?" Sun asked.

"You said Walter 'is' a good man. Not 'was.'"

Sun smile, it was a small wistful thing. "Well..." she began and looked around. "I've had a long night. Can we please sit?"

Mary nodded shyly and sat in an armchair and Sun sank into the couch with a sigh. "God, I hate night shoots. I think I'm just about too old for it."

Mary smiled but didn't say anything.

Sun leaned forward toward Mary, her elbows on her knees. "Walter is still a good man because he is out there, even as a ghost, helping people," she said. "I play a detective, but he has really become one."

"You are proud of him," Mary said. It wasn't a question.

Sun sat up and nodded. "Walter wanted this," Sun said, gesturing at the small trailer and all it implied. "He was good enough. He worked hard enough. He just wasn't lucky enough. I'm glad he's getting a second chance to do something..." Sun broke into a broad smile. "Well... something more important than all of this."

There was a weariness in Sun's voice that I wasn't used to. She had wanted the acting career even more than I had, had been even more driven and even better at her craft. Maybe it was all the years on the same show that had worn her down.

There was a knock on the door and a young man entered the trailer. "We're ready for you, Ms. Parker."

Sun nodded and smiled at Mary. "This shouldn't take too long. Wait for me?"

Mary smiled. "Of course."

And then Sun was gone and I would have followed her but for Mary.

"I know you are here," she said, her voice just above a whisper, her tone sharp, her lip curling a bit when she said "you."

Emily looked at me, her eyes wide again, her grip on my arm tightening, but neither of us spoke, like we were children hiding from our parents.

"Listen to me, Walter. You too, Emily." She opened up her purse and pulled out a gun. "You could fly off and go get the police, but if I hear a siren approaching, I'm going out there and I'll start shooting. I'm an excellent shot. Sun will die first."

I didn't know where we were. I hadn't left the trailer. I hadn't seen much but trees out the window and door. But from what she was saying we had to be fairly isolated. But that didn't mean law enforcement couldn't approach quietly.

"Don't leave, Walter," she said, slowly getting up. "You really don't want any more of the living involved in this." She unzipped her jacket and underneath was a vest with blocks of this grey play-doh-looking substance with wires and a single red light. "If this thing starts going the way I don't want it to… boom."

She said it dispassionately, without emphasis, and that made it all the more scary.

Emily squeezed my arm harder and I knew she must have so many questions, but neither of us spoke, terrified we might miss something.

"There's nails in the vest," she said. "A lot of people will be hurt. But look on the bright side, you might end up with some new ghost friends to help you go solve murders."

She zipped up her jacket and slowly smiled, looking all around the room. "Now, I need you to prove to me you are here. Flash the lights twice or something. If you don't, I'll go end this right now."

But I couldn't flip the lights on and off. It was within the realm of possibility, some ghosts could do it, but I couldn't. I had never tried.

She looked at her watch. "You've got two minutes."

"Can you?" I asked Emily, panic edging into my voice.

Emily shook her head. "JJ can," she said.

"Go get him! Go get Banquo. We need all the help we can get."

She nodded. "What are you going to do, Walter?" She was eyeing me like she thought I might try to do something crazy. And I might, but my mind was still too disorganized to even come up with a crazy idea.

"Better get a move on," Mary said.

"Please!" I said to Emily, and she popped away, leaving me alone with the killer.

84

Chapter Nineteen

I KNEW HOW JJ LYNCH HAD MANAGED TO TURN ON lights. He had lowered the frequency of his ghostly form in just the right way, put his hand into the light switch, and bridged the gap. That had allowed electricity to flow.

JJ had done a lot of crazy things with electricity. He had accidentally killed a man that was about to kill his best friend. He had spent the early part of his afterlife figuring this stuff out. I had less than two minutes.

It wasn't going to work.

And then I thought about the SECI chamber, this typewriter for ghosts. I have to lower my frequency and keep it lowered so it can detect my presence. Manipulating electricity was the same thing, lowering your frequency, albeit at a greater degree.

I had to try. What else was I going to do?

Ghosts emanate high-frequency electromagnetic radiation. It's how we see each other. That frequency is so high that the living can't see it. The SECI chamber has the best detectors they can get, but there is still quite a distance between our natural frequency and that. And even more to affect electricity.

"Ninety seconds," Mary said dryly.

Being an actor was all about faking things convincingly. I had acted my way into being a detective. Back at the university, I had had enough focus to pop. And doing things as a ghost is all about willpower, all about believing you can do something.

So I started acting like I knew what I was doing. I took my right hand and lowered its frequency to what the SECI chamber required. It's a feeling, not one I can really explain, because the biology of the living makes something this subtle hard to understand.

It's unnatural, it's difficult, it takes focus and you feel... I don't know, a quieting in your being. A slowing. So I took my hand down to SECI levels and just kept going.

I moved to the small kitchenette. It had a light above the sink that wasn't on. I lowered the frequency of my hand some more, slowed it down some more. Not my whole form, that would be too hard, just the hand.

"Sixty seconds," Mary said.

Where was Emily with JJ? He could do this easily. I felt my progress falter and then reverse some and I shook it off. If JJ got here, he could do something, but he wasn't here.

For Sun. I could do this for Sun.

To save her from this murderer.

The spark reignited and I used that energy to slow my hand down, to lower the frequency, to make it do what I needed it to do.

I stuck my hand in the switch and... nothing.

"Thirty seconds," she said. "Come on, Walter, surely you can figure this out."

I ignored her and focused. This was a mental game. This was willpower. I had a font of anger and desperation to fuel me. I was an actor and was used to pretending I knew what I was doing, which was effective a lot more than you think it would be.

I lowered my frequency more until my hand started to feel more solid, more substantial.

I tried again… nothing, but I almost felt something, a whisper of a sensation so dim I can't even describe it.

Frequency is so important as a ghost. If one ghost is to touch another they must be at similar frequencies or else they would just go through each other.

Frequency matters to the SECI chamber.

Frequency matters to electricity, which is another form of electromagnetic energy, just like I am.

It clicked in my mind and I suddenly wasn't faking it anymore. I really understood what I was doing. I just had to find the right frequency just like I did naturally now when I picked Emily up, but it was so hard at first.

"Ten seconds," Mary said, but her voice had changed. There was this sadness there, this tone of defeat.

That didn't matter. I tried again and… I definitely felt something, like the zing of a nine-volt battery on your tongue. I liked the feeling. I felt more alert.

I kept going. I knew how to do this. I just had to put enough energy into it, and for Sun I would do anything.

"Five… four…"

I tried again, the zing was stronger, almost too strong, but nothing.

"Three… two… one…"

I tried one more time… and the light flickered on and I felt a jolt run through me that was like… oh God, it was uncomfortable and horrible and so energizing. I loved it. I wasn't into cocaine or meth, but I have to imagine it was something like this. The addict in me woke up and smiled.

I removed my hand and the light went off and I missed

the jolt of energy. I put my hand back in and it went back on.

Mary was talking but I was so distracted by this feeling that I almost missed it. "...I'm so relieved. Oh, thank God, Walter, I was so afraid that I did all this and you weren't really here. That I was fooling myself with the odd tone I heard on the police scanners last night, and it wasn't you and Emily that found the body."

She sank into the chair, tears flowing down her cheeks.

Her hands were shaking and she rubbed at her face. Not thinking, I pulled my hand away from the switch and the light went out. I missed the feeling of the electricity, but this was more important.

"What are you talking about, Mary?" I asked, even though I knew she couldn't hear me. The electricity running through me was kind of like an extreme caffeine buzz and it fed the anger and the rage. "What the hell are you talking about!"

"I mean," Mary went on, "it wasn't easy finding that girl and getting her out there this morning, setting the second arrow up for you. Breaking into the union and putting the poster up. All in conjunction with Sun being here for this shoot. It all had to go perfectly. I... I can't believe that it did." She was looking around the trailer, her eyes trying to find me, but I wasn't visible to her.

She was babbling now, in between her tears. She wasn't right. She wasn't stable. She had done all of this to get me here, to be with her.

"I moved up here, to Flagstaff, after you died," she said. "I know you don't remember that night... the propofol took the memory away... and I... I guess that was for the best. I'd be in jail otherwise. I wouldn't be here now with you."

She dug into her right sleeve and pulled out a small

black switch about the size of a roll of quarters and held it in her hand. "I'm glad you're here with me, Walter. Today's the day that I join you on the other side. It's only right that you are here."

She took a deep breath and pressed the red switch on top and... nothing. Just a small click, and I realized what it was. A dead man's switch. This was far from over.

And then slowly, haltingly, she told me how I died.

Chapter Twenty

"I WAS IN LOVE WITH YOU," MARY SNIFFED AS SHE PACED the trailer, occasionally looking out the windows, which I was doing too.

The travel trailer was parked in a large lot that had a few other trailers set up, a semi, and a few cars. There was a small rustic-looking building fifty yards away and beyond that pine trees with some aspen groves. After a few looks, I recognized it as the cross-country ski area. We were outside of Flagstaff a ways, on the road that went to the Grand Canyon and was quite isolated.

I could see some white tents set up in the woods a couple hundred yards away, but there was no movement near us.

"And you never noticed," Mary continued. "Sun, Sun, Sun. It was always Sun. You thought of nothing but the past."

She walked to the door and peered out and then turned around, leaning against the door with a sigh.

"Look at me, Walter," she said, slapping her free hand against her chest. She was sweating and had unzipped her jacket showing a bit of the C4 strapped to her chest. "How's a girl like me supposed to compete with her? With the memory of her? With the perfect life you think you would have had but for that traffic accident."

Mary's tone was shrill, her eyes a bit too wide, her movements sudden and unpredictable. I had seen many sides of Mary in the five years we worked together, but not this side. I had seen depressed Mary and elated Mary and sad Mary, but not manic Mary.

"The truth is, Walter, you needed me. I wanted you, because you were a kind, handsome man in an unkind world. Because you really cared for your patients. Because you were so gentle. But you were so lost. I may not be skinny. I may not be beautiful, not like her, but all I wanted was to love you, to be with you, and you… goddamnit, Walter, you were so damn dense you couldn't take a hint."

Tears rolled slowly down her cheeks. "I gave up on you, after three years, I gave up. I met Ian and I was so glad to have a man interested in me that I didn't see how wounded he was."

She nodded her head slowly. "I know you want me to tell you what happened that night, fill in the blanks of how you died. Because I'm your unfinished business. I'm what's standing between you and your blissful afterlife. But isn't this perfect, Walter? When I was alive, I would tell you all my problems and you would kindly listen and try to help and I would fall a little more in love with you and you wouldn't even notice.

"Sixty-two months, Walter. That's how long we worked together. Sixty-two months. And you never really saw me, saw what I felt, not even once."

She had cut her victims sixty-two times on each side to commemorate each month she had loved me and each month I had missed it.

I wanted to leave. I didn't like seeing Mary like this. I didn't want to know how I died anymore. I just wanted to escape her, but I couldn't.

I had been stupid and obsessed with Sun. All those years after our divorce, I could hardly see another woman. I tried dating, every once in a while I would try, but it was always horrible and my heart was never in it.

Sun was my dream woman and acting was my dream job and I had treated my life after that as a consolation prize, as a defeat, as a reminder that I had almost had it all.

My profession. My practice. My life. All of it was a consolation prize.

"And now I die and Sun dies with me," Mary said, zipping her jacket back up and sitting on the couch so she could see the door. The knuckles of her right hand went white as she gripped the dead man's switch and a bead of sweat trickled down her forehead.

And now Mary was going to kill Sun and I was a ghost and I could do nothing to stop it.

Chapter Twenty-One

MARY WAS SO SHY WHEN I FIRST MET HER. SHE CAME TO her interview at the newly rented, but not yet furnished, offices of Hollywood Dental dressed in a tan skirt and a green blouse buttoned all the way to her neck.

She didn't look comfortable, not at all. She didn't make a lot of eye contact, but she knew her stuff. She had fought in Afghanistan and had more medical experience than the other candidates I had seen. She graduated at the top of her class, and if she survived being an army medic, she could handle a root canal.

But none of that is why I hired her. Well, I did hire her for all of those reasons, but that wasn't the deciding factor.

The deciding factor was that she wasn't my type. At all.

She was pretty in her own way and gentle when I had her examine my own mouth. She spoke thoughtfully and articulated herself clearly, but I wanted to avoid the possibility of falling for any of the women I hired.

I still held out hope for Sun even though it had been over two years since our divorce.

And while Mary and I were friends, while I would

ROBERT J. MCCARTER

listen to anything she wanted to talk about, I never fully opened up to her. I couldn't. She was an employee.

There was another candidate that was better than Mary, but she was thin with long black hair and brown eyes and quite beautiful. I couldn't have someone with me every day that reminded me of Sun, that I would try to make into a new Sun, so I hired Mary and shoved her so firmly into the little sister zone that I was blind to what was going on.

"So I married Ian," Mary went on, much of the energy out of her voice now. "He had served in Iraq. He knew what kind of nightmares I had because he had them too. We understood each other, but we couldn't help each other." She leaned forward, putting her head in her free hand. "But you know all of this, Walter. He was an angry drunk and he started getting drunk more and more. We fought. He wanted me, but we were not good for each other."

I did know all of this, she had confided in me over the years and I had been sad for her, I had tried to tell her she deserved better, but it hadn't been enough.

"He hit me," she said, her voice barely above a whisper now. "That's the part I didn't tell you. Not anywhere people would see, but he hit me... almost from the beginning."

She was crying. "After I got pregnant, he changed, for a little while, he changed. I thought it was going to work, but..."

The seconds flowed by and she sniffed. I was afraid for what was coming next. I didn't know what it was going to be, but I knew it was going to be bad.

When she raised her head, her eyes were hard and her nostrils were flaring. "But I couldn't stop thinking about you, Walter. It's you I wanted in bed with me, a kind,

94

gentle man. It's your baby I wanted to have. You were so happy and so damn supportive when I told you I was pregnant. I knew you had wanted to be a father so badly. I became more and more convinced that I had the wrong husband and that I was having the wrong man's baby."

She sighed and leaned back on the couch. As she talked, I kept looking out the windows, seeing if there was any movement close. What if her thumb slipped off the dead man's switch? Sun would be coming back after the shoot was done. What then?

"But you were kind and supportive and didn't have one damn clue as to how I felt." She dug in her pocket and pulled out her phone and swiped a few times and held it up. On it was a baby, maybe a year old, with thin brown hair and chubby, happy cheeks. "I never told you, but his middle name is Walter."

I stepped back and heard the whisper of the bardo. It told me this was going to get worse, a whole lot worse, and if I just let go, if I just sank into it, I would never have to know.

"But… he's not mine anymore," she said, her voice shaking. "After you died… I wasn't okay." She barked out an awkward laugh. "I guess it was that, but not *just* that. You had died and I… I had helped you." She shook her head. "Even after I did it, did what you asked, you still couldn't see me."

The call of the bardo got louder. She wasn't clear in what she was saying, but it was clear that it was going to be bad for me.

"That night, Ian and I had a big fight. Over you. He had finally figured it out, proving himself to be at least a little less dense than you when it came to me." She got up and started pacing, gesturing with her hands. I began hoping that her finger would slip, that she would kill herself before Sun got back, while no one else was close enough to get hurt.

"So I left little Walter and drove to the office. You were still there. I told you everything, and you…" she stopped pacing and by some twist of fate she stopped right in front of me and was looking right at me. "And you lost your shit, Walter." She barked out another laugh. "I had no idea you were as wounded as the rest of us. I thought you were the one person who actually had it together. You had given up gambling and propofol. The practice was doing good. But no, it turns out you were just acting."

She shook her head. "And the damnedest thing is that it just made me love you more. You muttered stuff about me being your little sister, how you could never look at me that way, how I would have to find another job."

She started pacing again. "I still had my baby weight and was heavier than normal. I thought that was it, that if I was just skinny, that if I dyed my hair black, that you would love me. I promised you I would change. I begged you to think about it. I kissed you and you acted like the touch of my lips was poison. And then… I got mad."

The bardo sang to me loudly and this time I knew what it was offering wasn't a complete lie, but I ignored it. I couldn't look away now. I had to know.

She went back over to the couch and slumped down. "But you know what, Walter? The propofol was your idea. You told me, 'I have to forget, Mary. I have to forget. If you really love me, you'll help me forget.'

"It was stupid. You weren't making sense. But then you were in the supply room jimmying open the cabinet, your hands shaking like damn leaves. You kept muttering about Haley, about how you were so stupid, about how you didn't know anything. You told me you had just talked to Sun, that she was with some Hollywood guy and you couldn't stand it. You took a vial and a syringe into the room with the big mural of Marilyn Monroe with her white skirt flaring up over the grate. You got in the chair, but your hands were shaking too bad, so you asked me to do it."

She took a deep shuddering breath. "You asked me, Walter. You asked me to help you forget what I had said when I bared my soul to you. You asked me to help you." She shook her head. "And I did, Walter. I helped you."

Chapter Twenty-Two

WHAT MARY SAID DIDN'T BRING BACK THE MEMORY, NOT exactly, but I could see it in my mind. I could see her so scared and vulnerable, dressed in sweats just a month into her new life as a mother pouring her heart out to me.

I didn't like it, but I could imagine my reaction that day. Mary was important to me. She worked with me day after day and I had badly missed her when she had been gone. I cared for her and I knew she cared for me, although I had put that tightly in the sibling column and had from the beginning.

It had been a hard day. My misinterpretation of what Haley wanted from me, the call from Sun about her relationship. And then Mary on top of that broke me enough that my addiction took over.

Looking at it without biology and all the chemicals that come with it, I don't have as much empathy for myself as I might. But I do understand. Addictions, just like the bardo, can get to a point where you just can't say no. It's about resisting in small ways frequently, not one big act of willpower.

"'Please,' you said from the pale blue dental chair," Mary said, "your brown eyes so freaked out. You had managed to load the syringe but you could barely hold it. 'My hands are shaking too much, you do it.' I should have said no, but I didn't. You told me how much propofol to use, but it sounded like way too much, I argued you down to half."

Tears started running down her cheeks. "I asked you what happened with Haley and you told me you thought the little bitch had a crush on you, but it turns out she only wanted to keep her job. You told me that you knew Sun was gone for good and it was too much to bear. And…" She paused, her chest heaving, her head in her free hand, but hardly a sound coming out of her. "I was so mad, Walter. So mad."

With her free hand she beat on the couch, dust puffing out in ghostly plumes. She didn't do it once or twice, but over and over.

"I came there offering you what you wanted most, Walter. I came offering you love from someone you already cared about, from someone you already loved on some level. I came offering you a lifelong companion." She continued to beat on the couch rhythmically. "I came offering you me… and… and… you could only grieve the loss of your wife, the perfect Sun, and your misunderstanding with the skinny, way too young for you, Haley."

She stopped, hunched over, panting.

I realized that this was a confession. Mary was confessing her sin to me, explaining it to me. This was Mary's last confession. She had no intention of living. And that made her very, very dangerous.

"So I pushed the amount of propofol you asked me to," she said, sitting up, her voice low and quiet. "I saw your face relax when it hit you, that little moment of ecstasy. And do you know what you did then?"

I didn't know and I didn't want to know, but it was too late to turn away. Too much was at stake.

"You said, 'Thank you, Mary. Thank you. I do love you, you know. I love you like the sister I never had.'"

Mary slapped the couch once, a plume of dust rising into the air. "You told me that like it made it all right. Like being loved like a sister when I clearly had much more complex feelings for you would be enough to make me feel better, so I…"

She bit her lip, her eyelids fluttering rapidly. She swallowed hard and said, "So I pushed the whole damn syringe without even really thinking about it. You smiled, so big you smiled, the words 'thank you' on your lips, and then you passed out. And then you stopped breathing. And then you…"

The room was suddenly silent, too silent.

When I had resolved to find my murderer to deal with my unfinished business, I thought it would be something clean, something simple, something understandable. Not this mess of bad luck and human frailty. Not this unintended moment where Mary just did a little more than I asked.

And that's the key here. I asked for it.

Emily, with her murder sense, hadn't been wrong about me. The act of another person had caused my death. But it wasn't that simple. I had fallen to my addiction. I had convinced Mary to help me use again. I had done this.

In that moment, I knew that I had been wrong about why I was an earth-bound spirit. I thought my unfinished business was solving my own murder. It wasn't. It never had been.

My unfinished business is about me, about the choices I

made and how I lived my life after it fell apart, looking back, not looking forward. It's not about being the victim of one terrible moment in Mary's life.

"I wasn't all right after you died," she said, her voice slow and her words thick. "After I killed you. I tried, I tried so hard to put it behind me. To find a way to be okay with Ian and baby Walter. To move on. But it was too much for me. I kept having dreams about that last smile on your face. You see, it wasn't a good smile, not a smile of a happy person. It was a smile of relief, of addiction, of forgetting.

"And I couldn't forget." She paused and took a deep breath. "I lost my job at first—Dr. Wheeler liked Haley better anyway. I lost my baby next. I wasn't stable. I did things. Ian left me, took the baby, got full custody.

"I did what you asked me to do, Walter, and I lost everything. There is nothing in this world for me anymore. But you, Walter. You didn't stay dead. You started writing, and I knew when I started reading your words that it was you. That it was real. That there was life beyond this." She slapped her chest, sweat trickling down her forehead. She must be hot in that jacket this long.

"So I read everything you ghosts were writing. I plotted and I planned and I…" Her voice broke and what came out was something of a cackle. "And I did some really bad things, but here you are, Walter. It worked. I'm so relieved it actually worked."

She stood up, a smile on her face, and I had to imagine that it was as disturbing as my last smile. It was the smile of a mad woman that was about to get what she wanted.

"And now, Walter," Mary said, looking out the window behind the couch where in the distance I could see movement. "Now Sun and I will be joining you in the afterlife and we can all sort this out there together."

Chapter Twenty-Three

I SCREAMED FOR EMILY. I NEEDED HELP. I HAD NO IDEA what was keeping them. It seemed like it had been hours since she had left, but it couldn't have been more than fifteen or twenty minutes. But that was long, too long. Had something happened to Emily?

Mary was still talking, going back over what she had already said, but I didn't care anymore. I knew the truth. I knew the huge part I had played in all of this when I was alive and since I've been dead.

There was guilt, tons of it, but that had to wait on the sidelines. It wasn't quite time for its big scene. We were at Mary's endgame and I had to stop her from killing anyone else.

I flew fast through the trailers around me and found them all to be empty. I flew out to the tents, out where they were shooting, and I saw Sun standing over the fallen body of a man in an aspen grove, the green leaves making a pleasant sound in the morning breeze.

The man was on his stomach, splayed out on the ground on top of layers of decomposing aspen leaves.

That was an actor, he would get up when the scene was over, but the similarity to the bodies that brought me here was striking and bizarre.

Sun looked disheveled and hurt, but resolute, her brown eyes narrowed as she looked into the distance.

Behind her, the sun was just coming up over the grey hump of Humphreys Peak, the yellow light spiking down and warming her face. They had three cameras on her from different angles back about twenty yards and two drones buzzing overhead. You had one chance a day to get a shot like this and they weren't taking any chances.

This was a hero shot, showing Sun's character, Melissa Lee, after the trauma that had befallen her, leaving the viewers with hope that she would find a way and would eventually get over this and be okay.

If only it was like that.

Her show was a good one, they would have some follow-up on her difficulties coping, but it would still make it seem easy when it wasn't.

But that moment, looking at a worn but still strong Sun, filled me up. It was Hollywood fakery, but it was just what I needed.

This thing wasn't a movie or a TV show. This was life and death. Behind me I had Mary wanting to die and in front of me I had Sun still vibrant and strong, the morning sun shining on her tired face as she looked towards the future.

I knew what I had to do. It was terrible, but it was clear.

Chapter Twenty-Four

Mary Paulson was sick. That was the only way I could look at it. I knew her, she wasn't a bad person, but she had broken. Her time in Afghanistan, her postpartum depression, and me… basically talking her into killing me. All that had broken her.

My death wasn't a suicide, that was not my intent. It wasn't a murder, that wasn't Mary's intent, not really. It was just a terrible moment as this world frequently creates.

And now to salvage this mess, I had to create another terrible moment. One I didn't know I could recover from, but I was determined that no one else die today. No one else besides Mary, that is.

"That's a wrap!" the director called, a middle-aged man with greying hair. "Great job, Sun!"

Sun sighed, her shoulders falling and the fatigue returning to her face in full. The body below her stirred, a Hollywood-handsome man I didn't recognize grinned up and Sun and said, "Glad that's over—being dead is so boring."

If I had the time, I would have snorted at that, death

had been anything but boring for me. But time was what I didn't have. I flew fast back toward Mary, back toward the trailer, and halfway there, I heard a "pop" and Emily was there.

Her eyes were wide and her usually perfect blond curls were disheveled. "Sorry, Walter. I'm…" she looked around the forest realizing we weren't in the trailer with Mary. "Galt and his boys were harassing JJ and it got serious and…" Her eyes narrowed as she studied me. "What's going on, Walter?"

My mind reeled. I knew if I told Emily what I meant to do that she would try to stop me, but there was no other way. "We don't have much time," I said. "Sun is back there. Stay with her. If she comes this way try to stop her."

"How?" Emily asked, her brow furrowing.

"I don't know! Just do something. We don't have much time. Please, Emily. Please stay with Sun for me. She…" I felt tears coming and I could have stopped them, but I didn't and they rolled down my cheeks. I needed Emily to listen to me. I needed her to stay away, because while I was sure a human wouldn't survive what was about to happen, I had no idea what it would do to a ghost, and I couldn't have this day ending with Emily hurt or worse.

From her disheveled appearance there was clearly a story about her and JJ and Galt and his boys, but I didn't have time for it. I didn't have time for anything. Sun was already walking this way.

"Okay," she said slowly. "I'll… I'll think of something."

I flew back towards the trailer and quietly said, "I love you, Emily." I knew that Emily with her excellent ghostly hearing could hear it. I knew it would make her wonder and doubt. But I was done not saying the things that needed to be said.

Chapter Twenty-Five

MARY WAS LOOKING OUT THE WINDOW AT THE PEOPLE slowly walking towards the trailers when I got back. Her face was red and her hand holding the dead man's switch was white knuckled.

"...all your fault, Walter," she was saying. "You know that, don't you? If you had just blown me off like a normal person and not freaked out and gone for the propofol." She shook her head. "When you got the screwdriver and went to the locker, I told you that Midge would quit. That you would lose everything. And you looked at me and I remember your eyes. Not the soft lovely brown they usually were, but your pupils were dilated like you were terrified, and you said, 'I'll replace it. She'll never know.'"

Mary sank back down onto the couch and sighed. "You should have just told me you met someone, Walter. Or lied and said you once had feelings for me but buried them away when I met Ian. Or..." she trailed off with a sigh.

She was mad. She was ranting. She was blaming it all on me and I had to agree with her on that one. I stopped listening. I went back to the light switch above the little sink and started lowering the frequency of my hand like I had before to switch on the light.

I took it down to SECI chamber level and kept going. I felt my body slowing down, like it was thickening. I did my best to not think about the minute or two I had before Sun would be too close. I tried to tune out Mary's babbling and blaming. I tried to not think about Emily and what would happen if she got too curious about what I was up to. And I tried to not worry about what would happen to me.

A ghost's form is this localized emanation of very high-frequency EM energy. What is a ghost beyond that? I don't know. A faded ghost is just gone, like when Emily couldn't pop to Anna-Maria. But what would happen to a ghost that was in the middle of an explosion when those forces ripped through the localized emanation of EM energy that is a ghost?

It was those thoughts that I tried to let go of. Tried to not worry about. An explosion was going to go off, I was just trying to make it happen before any of the living or any other dead were here.

I put my hand into the light switch and… nothing. Damn it!

I could hear voices as the cast and crew approached.

Mary was crying. It was this half-hysterical, half-maniacal sound and it was getting to me. It was speaking to me, or maybe it was the bardo. It was telling me that this was my doing. That I had pushed her over the edge. That I was responsible for all of this.

I shook it off. I refocused. I ignored the voices getting closer. I lowered my right hand's frequency and put it in the switch and… the light flickered on.

"What…" Mary mumbled between the tears. "Walter? Are… are you trying to say something?"

I pulled my hand away and the light went out. Mary

got up and slowly walked to the kitchenette, her eyes red rimmed and her round cheeks stained with tears. "Maybe you just want me to know that you are here. That we will soon be together."

She stood in front of the sink and waved her free arm around and it passed through me and I felt a slight tingle. Mary had an electromagnetic field, just like I did. A much denser one, and I felt it. But I didn't want her touch. I didn't want anything to do with her.

"Not long now," she said, nodding out the window where Sun was striding over the forest floor towards us, maybe thirty yards away. I could see Emily walking next to her, looking up and shouting. "And you'll be able to tell me yourself."

I was out of time.

I looked at the woman next to me and it wasn't Mary Paulson anymore. It wasn't the woman I knew who was working next to me all those years. It couldn't be her. If it was, I couldn't do what I needed to do. This woman, her name was Mary, but she was someone so different I could barely recognize her.

I looked at my slowed down hand, it didn't really look any different, but it felt different. I bit my lip and I put my hand into the dead man's switch Mary was holding and... nothing.

Damnit!

I could hear Emily's voice getting closer, her shouting and pleading with Sun. I could hear the chatter of the rest of the cast and crew as they shook off the manic energy of a night shoot.

What was wrong? My hand was at the right frequency. I stuck it back in the light switch and the light flickered on.

"What is it, Walter?" Mary asked. "If you are trying to

convince me not to do this, it won't work. I am going to do this. Not much longer now."

I didn't look out. I stared at the switch in her hand. She held the button on the top down and that stopped electricity from flowing, that broke the connection. I didn't understand the electronics inside, but I tried. The switch was spring loaded, and if it popped up, a small piece of metal would complete the circuit. Below it two wires traveled to the switch. If I tore it apart, stripped the wires and joined them, then it would go off.

But this wasn't high-voltage AC electricity like the light switch. This was low-voltage DC electricity, battery powered. Maybe that was it. My frequency was good for AC but not for DC.

But what should I do then? Go up or go down with my frequency?

I had no idea, but I put my hand inside of hers so it encompassed the whole switch. I stopped thinking about it and tried to feel. When I was getting close with the light switch, I could feel the slight buzz of electricity.

Mary was babbling, her eyes far too wide, her knuckles white and sweat trickling down her face.

I could hear the people getting closer. I should have looked, but I couldn't. However close Sun was, it had to be better if the explosion went off in the trailer with her outside. I focused on the switch. I varied my frequency. I searched for the slightest feeling.

"I love you, Walter," Mary said, her voice suddenly calm. "Since the day we met, I have loved you."

It didn't matter. Nothing she said mattered. I went with the feeling and… there was a bright flash of light and I knew nothing.

Chapter Twenty-Six

I FEAR FOR THE FUTURE. ONE WHERE THE LIVING DO things to get the attention of the dead and where the dead are forced to do things to the living. Terrible things.

Mary Paulson died instantly when I completed the circuit and the C4 strapped to her exploded. The travel trailer didn't contain the explosion or all the bits of metal that flew out, but it got some of it, it slowed it down.

The fireball reached an adjacent trailer and several pine trees ignited. Bits of metal and wood whizzed out into the forest and the parking lot.

Sun Parker was fifteen yards away, tired and desperate for some rest. The flash of light startled her and then the concussion of the blast knocked her down, bits of debris flying right over her.

Emily was buffeted by it and shouted out my name. While it weakened her greatly, it had no other effect.

A production assistant by the name of Alan took a bit of metal in his chest, and an actress named Sally got a pretty serious head laceration.

And it ripped through my ghostly form and destroyed it.

And I was gone.

I can't tell you where I was because I don't know, but I believe it was the same place we go when we fade. It is a state where we know nothing. Complete unconsciousness.

It was only the tiniest of moments as the light flashed and the unleashed energy ripped through my ghost form, but I felt the darkness coming and I was glad. I was ready for the comfort of the void. I was happy to not be.

But I didn't stay gone.

Eight days, twenty-three hours, and five minutes later I came back. To the same exact place I had been, except I was hovering several feet over charred ground in the morning looking at the burned-out bit of forest.

"I'm so glad you are okay," Emily said, a worried look on her round face. She was sitting on the charred ground close by. Waiting for me.

Being faded for nearly nine days is a long time. There was good reason for her to wonder whether I was coming back.

"What... what happened?" I asked. At first the nothingness of being faded clung to me like a warm blanket until the cold winds of memory ripped it away. "Oh..." I gasped. "I... Sun. Is Sun okay?"

Emily nodded. "She's fine. They took her to the hospital and held her for observation overnight, but she's fine. Some minor hearing loss, but it could have been a lot worse."

I floated to the ground and gingerly walked over to Emily. My steps were careful and tentative. I wanted to act as human as possible after what I had done. I didn't want to go fast at all.

The lollipop on her T-shirt was its usually cheery red,

but that didn't match with the serious face I was confronted with. She wasn't showing her emotions and had it locked to its default color. Not a good sign.

"I love you, Emily," I said. I had said it right before I blew Mary up and I figured she had heard it, but it wasn't the right way to say it and it needed to be said.

She stood up and smiled, but it was low-wattage and tentative. Something wasn't right.

"Is JJ okay?" I asked. "Anna-Maria? What happened with Galt and them?"

Emily shrugged and it was a lazy thing as if she barely had the energy to move, which was never the case with a ghost. "JJ's fine. He was faded for a few days, but that's it. He ended up summoning the call and Galt lost one of his boys to it. Things are..." her face darkened and she shook her head.

I squatted down in front of her and reached for her hand but she took a step back.

"Mary?" I asked. It was just one word, but it held a lot. I was asking her if Mary had moved on or if Mary was a ghost.

Emily shrugged. "No one has seen her, but..."

I nodded. I had been faded almost nine days, who knows what the explosion would have done to a brand-new ghost.

"Then what?" I asked.

Emily shook her head, her blond curls bouncing, but even that seemed low energy. "After all of this," she began looking around the charred ground and trees, "there is a group of ghosts that want to shut down the SECI chambers. They want it to go back to the way it was. There are living that feel the same. Factions are forming. Equipment has been malfunctioning at Afterlife Communications."

I tried to take it all in, but my mind wasn't quite all

here yet. There are always those that resist change. It's natural. There are some that do so violently. And new technology always brings unintended consequences—like what Mary did to get my attention.

"And what do you think, Emily?" I asked, suddenly understanding a little bit of her mood.

"I don't know, Walter," she said, slowly, like she had to think about each word. "I think we were doing some good, but..." She shrugged and looked around again.

Ghosts fighting each other. A human murdering to get a ghost's attention. Factions forming among the dead over the SECI chamber. Equipment being sabotaged at Afterlife Communications. And Mary's status still unknown.

It was a lot.

But it wasn't enough to explain how restrained Emily was, how missing the four-year-old was despite her ever-present lisp.

"What else, Emily?" I asked.

She hugged her chest, her green eyes hard and searching me. "I'm mad at you, Walter, and I'm afraid for you."

My mouth opened but I couldn't find any words. Her delivery was so flat and devoid of emotion that I suddenly understood that she wasn't just mad, she was furious.

"You should have told me what you were going to do," she said.

"But..." I began, "you would have stopped me. You would have—"

She held her hand up, cutting me off. "No, Walter, I would have helped you. I would have shared the burden with you and..." she looked down at the ground and kicked at the dirt that her ghostly foot couldn't move.

"But I didn't know what the explosion would do to a ghost, I..."

She met my eyes again and hers were fierce. "I did know what would happen, Walter. And I thought you, of all the people here, wouldn't be treating me like a child when things got bad. Wouldn't be making decisions for me. Wouldn't be trying to take care of me." She sighed.

I suddenly felt hollow. I had treated her like a child. If it had been JJ, I would have probably told him what I was going to do and asked him to stay away. But I didn't do that with Emily. I misdirected her. I let her appearance dictate how I treated her.

"I'm so sorry, Emily," I said

She nodded. "Thank you, Walter."

"What now?" I asked.

She smiled but it looked painful. "Now I'm leaving, Walter. For a long time, I think."

The reality of it tumbled down on me. "She" was leaving, not "we." No more Emily who loves murder so much and Walter who just wants to complete his unfinished business running around solving murders. No more Walter and Emily.

"Where are you going?" I asked.

She shrugged. "I think I'll start with Paris and see where it leads me."

"I really am sorry, Emily," I said. "I really am."

She gave me another one of those painful smiles. "I know you are. You were doing your best in a very difficult situation, I just…"

"What?"

She sighed and shook her head. "I can't explain it, what it's like looking like this and being dead for so long. I can't explain what it feels like when everyone treats you the way you look, the way they think someone that looks like me should be treated. I…" Her eyes roamed around the damage of the explosion and then found mine again. "I just need to leave."

I nodded slowly. "Okay, Emily. I'm... I hope you find what you are looking for."

She smiled and this time it was a little more real. "I hope you do too. JJ said to tell you that if you are ready for the call, he's happy to help."

With a "pop" she was gone and I was left amongst the damage alone.

Epilogue

EVEN THOUGH I FOUND OUT WHO KILLED ME, MY unfinished business is not finished. In fact, I was so wrong about what it even was. It wasn't about dying from a propofol overdose in my dental chair, it's about how I lived my life after I lost Sun and my acting career, including how I participated in that overdose. It's about how I lived my afterlife always looking for a way out. It's about the conflict happening now in our world among the living and the dead and what that means when the SECI chamber pierces the veil. And it's now about how I lost my best friend Emily by treating her like the four-year-old she looked like and not like the accomplished, experienced ghost she is. By treating her like a child and not my partner and best friend.

I have a lot of work to do. I never took up JJ on his offer of summoning the call for me. I am not ready.

"What do you think?" I asked Anna-Maria as I paced around the corpse.

We were in downtown Tucson almost three months after Emily left, the yellowish sodium glow of the streetlights filtering into the dark downtown alley. The young man looked out of place. A tourist with flip-flops and a crisp new concert T-shirt. He was slumped against a dinged-up dumpster, a trickle of dried blood on his chin.

Anna-Maria had come back from her encounter with Galt and his boys more than a little angry. They had fought, although her passionate explanation hasn't made it clear what exactly had happened, but she ended up fading and came back angry and she needed something to do besides trying to get back at Galt. So, with Emily gone, I have been working with Anchor's Irregulars, doing my best to turn them into detectives in their own right.

Which seems kind of ridiculous. It's not like anyone ever trained me. Well, that's not true. Emily trained me to be what she called a "proper ghost" and channeled all the twisted emotions I was feeling when she found me into something useful.

Anna-Maria needed something to keep her busy, something to do, and so did I. So it was time for more ghost detectives running around solving murders.

She was dressed in her tight jeans and leather jacket, her raven's wing black hair pulled back into a ponytail, a look of concentration on her youthful face.

"No obvious wounds, just this bit of blood on his chin," she said, stooping down and examining him closely. "The concert let out two hours ago—this kid shouldn't have been down here."

The young man was Anna-Maria's age, so her calling him "kid" just made me smile. But, then again, Anna-Maria had lived a lot of life in her twenty years.

I could feel his soul stirring in the flesh that used to contain him. This was likely to be an easy case, at least in terms of how he died and who killed him.

"You got this?" I asked.

She looked up from the pavement where she was squatting, an uncharacteristic look of timidity on her face. She composed herself and nodded. "Of course, Boss. I got this. I'll go grab Blinky if I need backup. I know you've got a tough one up in Phoenix."

I nodded, but studied her a bit more wondering if this was what Emily had been like with me. Seeing if I had enough of a challenge to keep me engaged but not too much of a challenge that I would be overwhelmed.

Anna-Maria was not nearly as wet behind the ears as I was back then, but she tended towards overconfidence and brashness and that could just get you into trouble. I wanted her to be focused and challenged, but I didn't want her getting anywhere near the bardo.

Things are changing. Everyone knows it. The little ghost detective thing I'm running is, in part, to give the living a good impression of the dead, to show that we can contribute to society, that it is important to hear our voices and not shut them off.

That's right. I am now involved in a kind of a "ghosts are great" PR campaign. As I had been for the first few stories I wrote, even though I didn't know it then. I wrote these cases up and Tamara and Jin published them. People read them. They thought about death differently. They thought about the afterlife differently.

Solving the murders has always been the focus, but telling these stories is important too. It's not lost on me what happened with Mary. That some might do bad things based on what I write. I still wrestle with it, but I think the good outweighs the bad here. I have to think that the world will be better if the living know, without a shadow of a doubt, that death is not the end.

I want to go after Emily. I have been practicing popping and I can pop to Sun reliably, and the rest of the

Irregulars I can pop to occasionally. I figure Emily is important enough that I can pop to her too. But Banquo told me to let her be, to give her time. This is how she deals with being dead so long, she withdraws completely, isolates, and eventually comes back.

But how long will that take? A year? A decade? Longer?

Emily feels like my most important piece of unfinished business. I no longer think that a ghost's unfinished business is one thing. My view on this afterlife has changed dramatically. I now think we are ghosts so that we can become better people before we "move on."

And solving murders and mentoring Anna-Maria is part of that, but I miss Emily so very much.

"I got this," Anna-Maria said with a grim smile. "Really, Walter. You can go."

I nodded, giving the corpse one last look. The ghost would be separating soon and then she would have to start mentoring a brand-new ghost. I looked into her brown eyes and smiled. I could feel it. She was ready.

"Thank you," I said and flew off into the night.

There was another murder to investigate and a whole lot of unfinished business to attend to.

More Mystery?

WHAT COMES NEXT FOR WALTER AND EMILY IS currently a mystery to me. If you'd like to find out news on them or my other writing, join my email newsletter and never miss a thing.

In the mean time you might want to check out *The Blood of Carterville*, the first book in my new mystery series.

The Blood of Carterville

Carterville, AZ. Population: 286. People with powers: 198

Just a sleepy former mining town turned tourist haven in the mountains of Northern Arizona until the "incident." The meteorite that gave everyone in the town powers, but only while near Carterville.

Some people think that the

blood of Carterville bestows
powers, but when a tourist stabs police Chief Henry
Carter's best friend, everything changes.

Henry will do the unthinkable to save his friend. But
when the crime gets complicated, can Henry find the
culprit and save his town, much less survive?

From Robert J. McCarter, long-time Arizona resident
and the author of *Shuffled Off: A Ghost's Memoir*, comes a
mystery and a town you will never forget.

Get The Blood of Carterville now!

About the Author

Robert J. McCarter is the author of seven novels, three novellas, and dozens of short stories. He is a finalist for the *Writers of the Future* contest and his stories have appeared or are forthcoming in *The Saturday Evening Post*, *Pulphouse Fiction Magazine*, *Fiction River*, *Andromeda Spaceways Inflight Magazine*, and numerous anthologies.

His latest effort is a serialized novel called *Woody and June Versus the Apocalypse*, a story of adventure and love and taking things (even the apocalypse) in stride. Of his novel, *Seeing Forever*, Kirkus Reviews says, "Sci-fi as it should be: engaging, moving, and grand in scope."

He lives in the mountains of Arizona with his amazing wife and his ridiculously adorable dogs.

Find out more at:
robertjmccarter.com

Books by Robert J. McCarter

Walter Anchor, Ghost Detective Stories

- **Case 1: Detecting Haley** (also part of *Life After: Stories of Life, Death, and the Places in Between*)
- **Case 2: The Ghost Bride's Gift**
- **Case 3: A Long Hard Fall**
- **Case 4: Death of a Dentist**
- **Case 5: A Hollywood Kind of a Murder**
- **Case 6: The Red Arrow Murders**
- **Unfinished Business: The Cases of Walter Anchor Ghost Detective** (coming October, 2020)

For a complete list of Walter Anchor stories, go to RobertJMcCarter.com/WalterAnchor

Novels in the "Ghost's Memoir" world:

- Shuffled Off: A Ghost's Memoir, Book 1
- Drawing the Dead
- To Be a Fool: A Ghost's Memoir, Book 2
- Of Things Not Seen: A Ghost's Memoir, Book 3
- A Boy, a Girl, and a Ghost

For a complete list the "Ghost's Memoir" novels, go to ShuffledOff.com

The Woody and June versus the Apocalypse Series

Find out more at WoodyAndJune.com

The Neutrinoman and Lightningirl Series

Find out more at Neutrinoman.com

Other Novels:

- Seeing Forever

For a more information, go to RobertJMcCarter.com

www.ingramcontent.com/pod-product-compliance
Lightning Source LLC
Chambersburg PA
CBHW060938120626
46557CB00003B/1054